To Frederic[illegible]

Thank for all yo[illegible]
for the children.
God Bless you!

Pam [illegible]

Wolf Tracks

Pam Avis

ISBN 978-1-4958-2014-4 paperback
ISBN 978-1-4958-2015-1 eBook

Printed in the United States of America

INFINITY PUBLISHING
1094 New DeHaven Street, Suite 100
West Conshohocken, PA 19428-2713
Toll-free (877) BUY BOOK
Local Phone (610) 941-9999
Fax (610) 941-9959
Info@buybooksontheweb.com
www.buybooksontheweb.com

For Matthew

Acknowlegements

I would like to thank Janice Teague, Nancy Bushey, and the late Ray Hayes for their unending support over these last few years. To my first editors Josh Eason and Sarah Young. Thanks to Mary Vono for her editorial help, comments and readings. To Brittany ASMR for her ability to bring the story to life with narration and finally to my husband Ray, for his belief and committment in this work.

Contents

Preface *vi*

Prologue *vii*

1. The Wedding of the Wolves *1*
2. Never Good Enough *13*
3. Calvin *21*
4. Time to Say Goodbye *41*
5. Up, Up, and Away *58*
6. The Village *77*
7. Nightmares *94*
8. Lollipops and Witches *111*
9. The Dance *123*
10. Can You Hear Me? *145*
11. Never, My Love 160
12. The Beast *183*
13. Gone in the Night *193*
14. The Black Pit *206*
15. Believe *215*

Epilogue *234*

Bibliography of Music, as appears in text *236*

Preface

When my son was very young, while putting him to bed at night, he would often ask me to tell him "Wolf Tracks" again. Over the years, the story evolved, and finally I decided to write it, and it became a book for our family. Eventually, I began to tell the story to my grandchildren.

My grandchildren would often play the music referenced in the book and talk about the story, whether at home or while we were taking long rides together. Even to this day, when my grandchildren come to visit, they say, "Tell us Wolf Tracks again."

This book gave us a special connection and brought our generations together.

Though written for children, I hope all ages will enjoy it.

Some of this story is fictional, and some of it is true and based on real characters.

—Pam Avis

Prologue

Spring 2005

"Time to go!" Harry's mother called again from the bottom of the steps. "Come on! Step it up, I've got lots of things to do today, Harry!"

Harry could hear her tapping her long nails on the banister. He knew she was getting impatient again. "And your report for school had better be done," she told him again. "Leave it on your desk for me to look over this weekend!"

He quickly dug through his papers and put the stupid report on the desk so she could check it. Then he grabbed his stuff and all but flew down the front stairs. He had been counting the seconds until he could get out of that house and over to Grandpa's, where everything was fun.

"Coming!" he yelled, but she was gone.

Nine-year-old Harry D. Bella II walked out his front door with his overnight bag so full that the zipper would not close completely. He immediately noticed that it was exceptionally hot for this time of year.

Just then, the garage door opened and his mother walked out, smiling, "How about taking the Mustang today?" She didn't wait for his reply, and simply sifted through her purse for her keys and unlocked the door to her 1969 yellow Mustang convertible.

Harry was mortified. *Oh no,* he thought. Didn't she know how foolish he felt being seen in that old car? It appeared he didn't have any choice, and he wanted to get to his grandfather's house as soon as possible.

As they whizzed down the street with the top down, the wind blew his mother's hair in her face, and made his unruly dark hair stand straight up on end. He tried to push it down, but it blew right back up again.

I must look like a nut, he thought, beginning to sit as low as possible so that he wouldn't be noticed by any of the neighborhood kids who always had something to say about everything Harry did or didn't do, or wore, or said, and it usually wasn't anything he wanted to hear. The only one he trusted, out of all the kids, anyway, was Erthworm. Erth, as he called him for short, was Harry's very best friend. His real name was Erwin Woodward. Harry didn't know how he got that nickname, but over the years it had stuck. They were different in some ways. Harry was said to be tall for his age, and his mother was always telling him he was too thin. He also had dark brown hair that never looked right to him, and he liked to get it cut as short as possible when she would let him. His friend, on the other hand, was much shorter than he, with light brown, stick-straight hair that he only cut when he was forced. Erth knew all about Harry's life; the good, the bad and even his secrets, but he had never made Harry feel embarrassed or ashamed, the way some kids would if they found the least little thing to harass someone about. Erth understood him completely, and he understood Erth. They had vowed to each other to be best friends for life.

"Back in the sixties, they really knew how to make a car and how to make good music too—not like that junk that's on the radio today—with a few small exceptions," his mother said as she winked. She proceeded to turn up the volume even louder on the oldies station she listened to constantly, claiming that she loved the song they were playing.

Harry knew the song, the words, and who was singing it. He could tell you practically everything about the music of the sixties and seventies, because he had been saturated with it for so long. He had heard this song a thousand times. According to his mother, those were the days, and everything was better back then, at least as far as she was concerned.

Finally, they were pulling onto the main street, and he felt it was safe to sit up straight, thankful that no one had seen him. He no longer cared how loud she played her music or if the top on the old car was up or down. At last, he was on his way to spend the weekend with his grandfather, and he was thrilled.

He felt like yelling out, "Yippee, I'm outta here!" But, he decided to keep his mouth shut, which is mostly what he did around her.

His mother seemed exceptionally happy for a change as she drove along, singing with the radio. Harry glanced over at her as she suddenly began to belt out the *whah, ahh—ahh,* to "Close to You" by the Carpenters, and his eyes widened, surprised to hear her singing so loudly, especially in the morning. Anyway, she was happier than he'd seen her in a while, and he kept his fingers crossed, hoping she would stay in that mood, at least until they got to Grandpa's house.

"I bet you didn't know this was the song your father and I danced to on that special night when I first met him," his mother told him, her voice getting softer. She hummed along, and Harry looked at her and spotted a tear forming in the corner of her eye.

Harry felt sad for her again. Music affected her so much, bringing back so many memories for her. He guessed it reminded her that things would never be the same for her, now that his father was gone and remarried. Things were never the same for him either. Everything was different. Everything was worse, but he knew all too well that her mood could change in a heartbeat. Even though he was ecstatic about spending a whole weekend with his grandfather, he knew if he acted too excited, she would guess that he was going to have much more fun than he was allowed. So the trick, he decided, was to act as if it were any old day. Otherwise, the dumb old lectures would begin all over again as they always did, and Harry could just hear her now; first she would start with, "Now, listen, Harry, you are not to have any candy," and then the lecture would follow about teeth, dentists, and root canals!

From there, it would escalate into, "And don't you *dare* ask your grandfather for that Cherry Cola," and another lecture on nutritional values and bones and having his growth stunted.

The final clincher, and worst part of all, would be when she'd say, "We don't let Grandfather buy more things for you, do we? That means no prizes, toys or any more *junk* that would require your grandfather to spend money on you." Harry wouldn't say a word.

"Now, Harry," she'd say, looking at him, crunching her eyebrows together, "promise me," and he'd pretend he didn't hear her, and she'd say it again, louder, "Promise me, Harry!" and she'd crunch her brows together even tighter, until Harry would assure her. Then she'd look at him again until she was satisfied that he meant it.

"Okay, it's agreed then," she would drill him. "Under no circumstances will you ask for or even *hint* that Grandpa should buy anything for you." Harry would nod again, sadly, all his plans bursting within one simple, thirty-minute ride.

For the remainder of the ride, she would talk on about how this was all for his own good. Otherwise, he would grow up to be over indulged, irresponsible, and she'd go on adding that everything does not grow on trees, and enough was enough, and how was he going to support a family if he grew up thinking everything grew on trees, especially if he had to spend all the money he earned on his teeth? Still, she'd carry on until Harry began to count the minutes until he could get out of that car, hoping, all the while, that he could keep himself from screaming.

So, Harry had come up with a plan that morning, when his mother had come into his room to tell him to pack his bags because he was going to stay at Grandpa's for the weekend. Instead of yelling his usual, "Yippee, yahoo!" He'd just said quietly, without even looking up, "Oh, that's nice." She'd smiled and shut the door. As soon as Harry heard the door click shut, he banged his fists together and whispered excitedly to himself, "Yes!"

Matteus C. Bella II came sprinting out of the front door of his big old country house as soon as he saw the car pull into the driveway. Harry jumped out of the car and ran up the walkway, yelling, "Hi, Grandpa!"

Grandpa quickened his pace and smiled as he went to give his grandson a big welcoming hug. As Matteus walked toward the car, Harry's mother turned down the radio and smiled at her father in law. "Hi, Grandpa," she said.

"Susan," he said as he kissed her cheek. "You're looking wonderful!"

They had their usual chit chat, and Harry ran up to the car to give his mom a kiss goodbye. All she said was, "Be good for Grandpa," and she pulled out of the driveway, and they looked on after her, waving goodbye.

Harry was shocked—his plan had worked—no lectures, and, best of all, no promises that he didn't want to keep!

Harry and Grandpa hurried into the house, carrying Harry's bags and making plans for their day together. They put his stuff in the room Grandpa always kept just for him, complete with a video game player, roller blades, and other such items Grandpa thought he and Harry would enjoy.

Within five minutes, they were off to the country store, where they made every kind of candy in every shape and size. They each filled a bag with their favorites, then headed back home to play with Harry's new video game he had brought with him. Thirty minutes later, they were off to the toy store to find the player's guide that went with the video game. While they were in the toy store, they spotted a good-looking baseball and bat that they just had to have, too. They ate their candy as they drove back, Harry reading the guide in between bites, studying all the secrets to mastering the game.

Later, as lunchtime rolled around, they roasted hot dogs and drank pink lemonade while munching on handfuls of cheese curls.

After their meal, they went outside to the barn, and there was Harry's new black and yellow racing bike. His grandfather had bought it for his birthday, and it was only the second time he had gotten to ride it. There it sat, waiting for him, and sitting right next to it was Grandpa's bike.

Off they both went on their bikes, riding through the neighborhood. It was a beautiful spring day and the wind was blowing through their hair as they raced up and down the hilly town, feeling free as birds.

When they returned, the kids from down the street showed up, and it was game time. Grandpa said he would watch them play. They decided on a baseball game first. Next came a game of dodgeball, and then they even shot a few hoops in the driveway. For Harry, it was always more fun to play when Grandpa was watching. He'd cheer Harry on whenever he scored.

After a couple of hours of hard playing, the kids went home, and Harry, hot and thirsty, went in with Grandpa, and they each had a root beer and decided to play a game of Chess.

Grandpa watched Harry while he was in deep thought about where he should move his knight. He cherished his only grandchild and was concerned for him, as well. Harry's father moved 3000 miles away after the divorce, saying he couldn't give up this opportunity in his career to advance the jewelry business. He knew Harry only saw his dad for four weeks out of every year. He was amazed that Harry was doing so well and seemed happy, in spite of all the changes in his life. Grandpa lived alone since his wife had died five years before. Now it was important to him to make the most of his precious time with Harry. Remembering how much he had missed out in raising his own son, he knew he wouldn't make the same mistakes again with his grandson. He wished his son had listened when he tried to tell him that this is what matters; your family, and your son's childhood, but his son couldn't see it. He felt he had to further his career. Grandpa did not want to argue with his son. He knew he'd have to learn it on his own, as he had; the hard way, and with many regrets.

"What do you say we go to Sally's Diner tonight for dinner?" asked Grandpa.

"Yeah, can we get those double deluxe cheese burgers again, with the curly fries?" Harry asked eagerly.

Grandpa nodded, smiling, "Will you have room for dessert?"

"I'll make room for it," Harry said eagerly.

"Well, you let me know when you're hungry enough to eat, and we'll be on our way."

They played for about five more minutes and Harry said, "Grandpa, I'm starving." They were off to Sally's Diner. As soon as they arrived, they sat up at the counter, and Sally, herself, came over to greet them. She was an older woman, with lots of white hair piled up on her head, light green eyes, and a hardy laugh.

"Well, Harry," she said in her Irish brogue, "Aren't yer lookin' fit as a fiddle. I see yer just about all grown up." Harry smiled. He liked Sally. "Now ya tell me, what's a near grown up handsome lad like you want to eat for his supper tonight?"

Harry gave her the order, and she wrote it on the slip. Smiling over at Matteus, she said, "And I hope you, sir, are not even thinkin' of eaten that for yerself. We gotta keep that ticker of yours workin' up to par."

Matteus ignored her remark and began to order, "A double bacon cheeseburger—"

"Oh, holy Mary, mother of God, they'll be puttin' you in the ground by tamari mornin', eatin' all that junk food. No, sir, you'll have one tossed salad with light vinaigrette, ya will," she said, raising a stern eyebrow to Matteus.

Mattues frowned a little, "And an order of fries!" he announced stubbornly.

"And the broiled fillet of sole with a baked potata, hold the butter," she ordered as she wrote. "Perfect," she said. "Coming right up."

"Ah, you're worse than my late wife, may God rest her soul," he said, shaking his head.

"You'll thank me one day," she smirked. Then she spun around with her notepad. Harry could not help laughing.

"Hey, no laughing, or you'll get the same," said grandpa, smiling.

Harry covered his mouth and turned away. There was no arguing with Sally, he could tell.

They watched all the goodies that the waitresses were preparing behind the counter. Everything looked so delectable to Harry. He wasn't sure what he should get for dessert. Sally brought their dinners to them, their plates piled high. As they ate, Harry managed to smuggle a few coveted fries over to Grandpa when Sally wasn't looking.

Next, they ordered dessert. Harry decided on the peanut butter and chocolate sundae with marshmallow-whipped cream and Jimmies. Gandpa said to make it two!

Sally looked over and said, "Nice try. Let's see, that'll be one scoop of low-fat vanilla yogurt with fresh fruit toppin', hold the whippin' cream. Excellent choice it is, Matteus," she said, scribbling it all down. Then she spun around again, and this time, Grandpa stuck out his tongue at her as she walked away.

Harry couldn't hold back, and burst out with hysterical laughter. As Grandpa motioned to him to be quiet, Harry's laugh was contagious and Grandpa began to laugh too.

When they got home, it was back to the video game. After a couple of hours of secret passageways in hidden castles and fighting zombies, Grandpa said, "Harry, can you do me a favor?"

"Sure, Grandpa. What is it?"

Grandpa went in the kitchen and came back holding an apple. Harry looked up from his game. "You know your mother wants you to have healthy foods, right?"

Harry nodded.

"Why don't you eat this apple? Then I'll know you ate something that was healthy for you today."

"How," said Harry, "when I'm so full now?"

"Alright, how about a couple bites? You know what they say: somethin' about a bite a day—uh—keeps the doctors away." He shrugged.

Harry chuckled as he bit the apple.

"Good. Now I can relax, knowing at least one or two vitamins have gotten in there today," he said, pointing to Harry's stomach.

Harry stopped playing the game and looked over at his grandfather.

"What's wrong?" asked Grandpa.

"I need a break," said Harry.

"Oh, well, sure. We'll take a break." Grandpa told him.

"No, I didn't mean from the game, I was talking about at home. It just seems like I can't do anything without a lecture. It wasn't always like that, it use to be good when dad was with us," Harry looked down. "Anyway, what I really wanted to tell you is that I definitely decided I want to be in the music business. Music changes people for the better. The only time my mom lets up is when she's playing her music, which seems to calm her somehow and bring back happy memories or somethin'. And I guess sometimes sad ones too. I think I know just about every popular song from the sixties and seventies by heart, and a few country and western singers, and also some newer songs."

"Really?" asked Grandpa. "Just from hearing her play her music?"

Harry nodded. "Almost every night now since dad left, when she thinks I'm in bed, she takes out her wine and then puts on her old records. After a little while of listening to the songs, sometimes she starts to cry."

"How do you feel when you see her like that?" asked Grandpa.

"Well, the first time I saw her like that, I was really upset and sad. I watched her for a long time at the top of the stairs, but she couldn't see me. I promised myself that I would be a better son for her, do anything I could to help. But the next morning she came into my room and woke me up like nothing ever happened. I mean, it was like any other day. She started tapping that long fingernail of hers like she always does. She taps on the toothbrush holder, taps on the coat rack hook, taps on the light switch if I don't shut it off, and anything else that she can think of, if I should forget to follow the rules. Tap, tap, tap! That's all I ever hear, and, worst of all, that nail never breaks, it just keeps growing longer."

Harry looked frustrated and Matteus was quiet for a long moment, a look of concern on his face. He broke the silence. "People can have a time of sadness, and they may need that time. But, like everything, Harry, eventually it passes. People get over their loss and grief and they begin to let it go. What usually remain are the happy memories." He hesitated a moment and looked into Harry's eyes warmly. "I'll tell you what, Harry, if you can obey your mom, even though it may seem hard at times, when you come to stay with me, we'll make happy times for each other and enjoy being together, doing the things we like to do best, including playing music together. And we should make it as often as we can! That way, you'll get a lot of breaks."

Harry smiled as he spoke. "Well, I know that I want to be a radio Disc Jockey too when I grow up and everything else that has to do with music. I see how much music can change a person's mood from happy to sad, or sad to happy. I think that's a cool thing to be able to do for people."

Grandpa smiled and nodded in approval, "That sounds fantastic, Harry, really fantastic!"

"I bet things were better back in the olden days, like when you were a kid. I bet things didn't get so mixed up. It was an easier life, wasn't it?" Harry asked.

"You know, it's funny you should say that, because I've been waiting for just the right time to tell you the story of your great, great grandfather, Calvin."

"Wow!" Harry's eyes widened. "I didn't even know I had a great, great grandfather!"

"Yes, you did, and, well, his life wasn't quite so simple. He had his share of problems too, big problems, and some very scary and dangerous times, but it's how he overcame all of those things that made him so memorable," he told him.

"I'll tell you what, you get yourself ready for bed and give a holler when you're ready. Meanwhile, I'll go get the journals of Grandfather Calvin," said Grandpa, smiling. Harry jumped up and ran to his room. Grandpa yelled after him, chuckling a little, "And don't forget to brush those teeth! I just don't want them to fall out on your pillow tonight while you're sleeping, after all that candy we ate!"

Harry went as fast as he could, hopped in bed, and yelled out to Grandpa that he was ready.

Grandpa went to the bookshelf and took down the old journals that his great grandparents had kept all those years and passed on to him. He dragged his favorite rocking chair into the room and pulled it up next to Harry's fluffy bed. He opened the book and showed Harry the picture of Grandfather Calvin Bella when he was just a young man.

"Wow, how old is that picture?" asked Harry, quite amazed.

"Well, I guess it would be about a hundred years old."

Harry stared at the picture in awe. "Is that a real, live wolf beside him in the picture?"

Grandpa studied the photograph for a moment. It was the only one he had of his Great Grandfather Calvin, and there he stood beside the massive wolf. "The wolf, well, yes, that is a real wolf, Harry. And I guess that would be the best place to begin. But, Harry, this is not just a story. This is real, and as I tell you about your family as it was passed down to me, I want you to close your eyes and picture it; visualize it in your mind, smell the smells, hear the sounds, for it is quite a heritage that you have. I want you to be able to imagine what it was really like back then, okay?"

"Okay, I'll picture it, see it, and I'll even tell you the music it makes me think of. I'll listen hard so I won't miss a thing."

This gave Matteus an idea. "Harry, I'll tell you what, if a song comes to your mind as I read to you, I'll pencil it into the journal. After all, this was your family too, and if you have something to add, I want it in here. Who knows, maybe your children will read it someday."

Harry smiled, feeling absolutely elated that he could be a part of it. "I already thought of one song," he said, smiling.[1] "But just tell me first; did Great, Great Grandfather Calvin really know wolves?" he asked, his eyes filled with wonder.

"Oh, yes, he did," answered Grandpa, nodding his head. "He certainly did…"

---

[1] The Judds. "Grandpa"

1
The Wedding of the Wolves

Moona ran as fast as the wind through the thick dense forest, her pure white fur glistening in the sun, and her blue-topaz eyes, shining and bright. She was on her way home and she couldn't get there fast enough. She wanted to talk to her mother and tell her the exciting news.

As she ran, she remembered how she used to run home to her mother when she was a child, but most of the time she'd be crying. The other wolves always made fun of her because she was the only white wolf. Moona had felt so alone then, so left out. When she would tell her parents, they would always reassure her that she was special.

Moona would cry out to them saying, "I don't want to be special! I want to be like everyone else!"

"You have a very unique beauty and the others will see that in time," her father would declare. She certainly did not want to argue with him, but she could not even imagine that happening. She felt like she did not belong anywhere.

It wasn't until recently that she thought that they might have been right. But today, Kanodia had asked if she would go for a walk with him that evening. She could hardly hide her elation when he had asked. She had been hoping for this for a long time.

Kanodia was very handsome, dark and strong, with brown and golden eyes. He could run faster and jump higher than any other wolf in the pack. Many of the other wolves admired him. After all, it had been Kanodia who had stopped the hyenas from taking their food and crossing into what was known as "wolf territory." Worst of all, they had even attempted to steal their babies!

The hyenas were always trying some new scheme on the pack to get more from them. The wolves knew how dangerous they could be if not watched and controlled by a strong leader, but now that Kanodia was fully-grown and had proven so often that he was stronger than they were and completely unafraid of them, well, they soon grew afraid of him.

The more Moona watched him and learned of all his ways, the more she cared for him. "Yes," she said to herself as she neared her home, "he is the only one for me!"

When she arrived, her parents, Sasha and Dakota, were waiting for her. She quickly told them of her date with Kanodia, and they could tell she was happy by the look in her eyes.

"He is a fine choice, Moona," her mother said, her father nodding his head in agreement.

"It would not surprise me a bit if you find out that he feels just as happy to go out with you," her father said proudly.

"You really think so?" Moona asked joyfully.

"Of course, dear. Haven't we always said that you were very special? And you've grown up to be quite beautiful," her mother added.

She smiled with a look of pure glee on her face.

Well, she thought, *no one ever makes fun of me anymore, the way they used to.* Moona quickly put that out of her mind. She could hardly wait to see him again.

As if her parents could read her thoughts, her mother said, "Oh, darling, Father and I are so thrilled to finally see you this happy, and to find someone that you really care for."

Then her father added, "You'll find out, Moona, that I was right when I said he feels the same about you. Why, he'd be crazy not to. Anyway, honey, we are with you one hundred percent!"

Moona felt so grateful to have parents this wonderful, she looked at both of them for a long moment. "I love you both so very much," she told them, a tear brimming at the corner of her eye.

That night, Kanodia had arrived exactly on time. They ran through the forest until he found a quiet place for them to be alone and talk. The stars were out and it was a beautiful evening. They talked for hours about everything, and when he finally walked her home, he asked to see her again the next night.

They continued to go out every night, until one evening he asked her to come and watch him play bitterstick. This was a most important game to the wolves, because it proved your strength and how ferocious your bite could be.

Every five years, the wolves would have this competition. They would choose a tree with three strong, high branches on it. The first branch would be about eight feet off the ground. The second, ten feet, and, finally, the highest branch would be at least twelve feet high from the ground. The object of the game was to start at the running mound, build up speed and make your best jump, then bite the branch leaving a good set of teeth marks in it. If you could make the jump on the first branch, you would stay in the game and have a chance to get the second branch, and so on. If you did not make the jump and leave the bite on the first try, you were out of the game. The winner would become the new leader of the pack.

Three senior judges were appointed to make the decision as to which wolf would be their new leader. All the wolves would come from miles around to watch the big event. Even the hyenas would secretly watch them play so they would know which wolves to avoid.

Moona was one of the first to arrive and she waited anxiously in the front row to see Kanodia play. Only twenty-one wolves were qualified enough to even enter in the game. They began to take their place in line.

Now, all the wolves on the sidelines waited with great anticipation. The game began as each one tried desperately to make the jump and leave a deep bite. One after another made the attempt, but only seven out of the first twenty-one were able to stay in the game.

Finally, Kanodia, who had wanted to go last, stepped up to the mound. Then, he leapt off and ran toward the tree, jumped, and bit into the branch with ease. Then, something strange happened. Without even running again, this time he jumped straight up from underneath and bit into the middle branch, leaving a perfect bite.

The wolves howled at seeing this, as it had never been done before. Moona cheered as loudly as she could, and as she did her heart swelled with pride.

Kanodia drew back and waited until they were ready to conquer the highest branch. They all stood watching until there were only two finalists left. Now, it was time for the highest branch.

The first finalist was not able to make the jump; instead, he ended up bumping his snout against the branch giving out a loud *OUCH!* He stomped away when he heard the others laughing. They did not mean to laugh, but it was a funny sight. The next finalist, Manny, who thought he was the greatest, stepped up, ran, took the jump, and very cleanly and neatly sunk his big teeth into the highest branch.

The others gasped and howled and secretly began to make bets with each other as to which one they thought would win the game and become the new leader of the pack.

Manny, who adored an audience, put his tail straight up in the air and sauntered over to the sidelines, grinning at Kanodia as if to say, smugly, *beat that one.*

Kanodia, who loved a challenge, stepped up and stood on the mound for a moment, taking in a few deep breaths. There was not a sound, as most of the wolves that were watching stood motionless, holding their breath. Moona couldn't stand to watch, and squeezed her eyes shut, but curiosity got the best of her. All she could do was stand there, watching, frozen as she stared at him, praying he could somehow still win.

Kanodia looked calm and focused. He drew back and then, with all his might, he pushed off the running mound and then took the jump of his life. It seemed as if he had wings as he soared through the air. As he neared the high branch, he opened his fierce mouth and he bit into the branch with such force that his bite went all the way through it, sending the branch falling to the ground and landing right on Manny's head! As if that were not enough, he dropped gracefully to the ground.

The wolves went wild. They were howling and high fiving each other. The three eldest wolves that were the official judges announced that Kanodia was the winner. The shouts and the applause could have been heard for miles. They were clearly happy to have him as their new leader of the pack.

The judges asked him to stand up on the mound. As they walked toward him, they presented him with a crown and a scepter. The crowd whistled and applauded as they viewed the stone on the scepter. It was a huge, dazzling gem, and it sparkled like no other they had ever seen. Kanodia nodded to the crowd and thanked the judges. When they all calmed a bit, Kanodia humbly stepped down.

The crowd continued to cheer him until the judges nodded and they grew quiet. The judges read the age-old rituals and once again announced the duties and responsibilities of the leader. The judges spoke to the crowd also, saying that they expected all to cooperate and give their loyalty to their new leader, Kanodia!

The crowd let out a roar and yelled out, "Forever reigns Kanodia! Forever reigns Kanodia!" over and over again. As they cheered, it was as though they could be heard throughout the entire enormous forest.

As the night ended, Kanodia walked up to Manny and said, "Good game." But Manny was still angry about the branch falling on his head and losing, so he just gave Kanodia a mean sneer and walked off.

After watching the game from afar, the hyenas knew they didn't stand a chance of getting away with a thing, now that Kanodia was the new leader. They were sure if they tried anything he would finish them all off for good and banish them from that side of the forest forever.

They reluctantly went to find their leader, Beast, who was awaiting their report. He would not be happy about this at all, and they would all have to listen to him go on raging about it for hours. After all, if Beast was mad, they were all in trouble.

And trouble wasn't the word for it. Beast was furious. He called them *good for nothin' rodents*. He starved them. He made them watch him eat, then asked slyly, "Hungry, little rodents? Here have a bite," he said, taunting them. As the starving hyenas grew nearer, he dangled a piece of meat in front of their eyes. Their tongues hung out of their mouths and the saliva formed at the creases as they approached the daunting Beast.

Beast then brought the piece of meat up over his head and dropped it into his own mouth. Then, he immediately unleashed the longest razor-sharp nails they had ever seen and swiped at their heads. "Next time you won't let a leader like Kanodia get control, will you!" he roared. "I'm sick of them, sick to death of those wolves getting the best of everything! And I am even sicker of you good for nothing rodents who are incapable of ever doing anything right," he roared on, then he lunged to swipe his claws at them again. The hyenas, already starving and now bleeding, ran for their lives. They did not want to be strung up by their hind feet and left to rot for all to see, like they had seen their evil leader do to others many times before.

Kanodia felt he could finally slip away for a while and be alone with Moona.

"I'm so proud of you Kanodia, I don't even know what to say." Moona told him.

"Say you'll marry me," he asked softly.

Moona looked stunned, "Did I hear you right," she asked.

He whispered into her ear. "You are my one and only love. Please, Moona, say you will be my wife. You know even being their leader would not mean a thing to me if I couldn't have you by my side."

This time, though, still stunned, she knew she had heard him. She looked deep into his golden eyes. "You are my one and only dream come true. Now and forever, I will be your wife."

He drew his face up to hers, rubbing the side of her cheek. "So soft," he whispered, "so beautiful. I want to make you happy, the way you have made me." They both knew they could stay that way forever.

Moona still could hardly believe she was actually living her dream come true. *It was even better than I could have imagined,* she thought.

Kanodia walked Moona home, and she sat with him for a while before going in. They finally said good night, and she watched her husband-to-be run off into the forest under the full yellow moon.

Suddenly, out of nowhere, Evana appeared. Moona did not know what to say, as Evana kept her distance, yet she stared at her with a threatening glare. Moona could see her black fur shining under the moonlight, and those deep, green eyes glowing with jealousy. Then she remembered how much Evana had teased her as a child.

Moona waited. Evana said nothing. Moona thought, *too bad for you, then. Wait until you find out I'm going to be his wife.* Then Moona turned and left her still standing there.

They decided to marry as soon as Kanodia could organize his pack. He began by speaking to Manny. When Manny saw him approaching, he immediately felt embarrassed at how he had behaved during the game.

"Hey, Kanodia," said Manny meekly. "I'm sorry I was such a sore loser the other day."

"Sore loser or not, that was quite a jump you made at the game, and I came to ask you to be a part of my team."

Manny looked puzzled.

"You know, like second in command. When I am gone or busy, you will take my place. What do you say?" asked Kanodia again.

A proud look appeared on Manny's face, and he stood taller now. "It would be an honor," he answered making his voice deeper.

"Great," said Kanodia. "Come and see me tomorrow and we will talk over the details."

"I'll be there! You can count on me," said Manny.

Kanodia nodded with approval and took off like the wind. He found that he could run up to twenty miles now without even breaking a sweat. "It's because of Moona," he said out loud to himself, "she brings out the best in me." He took off even faster at just the thought that in one week she would be his wife.

Word spread like wild fire, and everyone had heard about the wedding of Kanodia and Moona. Many of the wolves wanted to help prepare for the big day. Soon, everything was in place for the wedding and not a detail was missed. Wildflowers of every sort were gathered and placed perfectly. The finest of foods were prepared. They even had made a necklace of flowers for Moona to wear around her graceful neck. The necklace was made of pure white gardenias that gave off a delicious fragrance all around her. The day had finally arrived.

Moona appeared beside her parents. They were elated for her and whispered again and again that she had never looked so lovely.

Kanodia stood proudly before all as his wife to be had come to stand beside him. Everyone agreed that they were perfect for each other. As the wedding took place, they celebrated under the moonlit night. It was an enchanting evening. They ate, drank, and danced under the stars, everyone having a wonderful time.

Kanodia had stopped for just a moment to look over at Manny, who was keeping watch for any nasty intruder that might want to upset their special day. Manny told him that he had caught a few pests trying to nose their way in, but a few growls from him and they had run for their lives. Kanodia nodded, pleased with him and feeling he had made the right choice as he went back to his lovely new bride.

Manny did not tell him that he had caught one of the hyenas trying to slip in and steal some food. Manny had seen them slither in from a distance while the others were all dancing. He waited until they were almost ready to snatch the succulent shank off of the wedding table. Then, Manny gave a ferocious roar, revealing rows of sharp teeth. None of the other wolves heard him, though, over the loud festive music of the wedding party.

Startled and afraid, the hyenas began to run, but Manny caught them in seconds. He stood up on hind legs and banged their heads together. Both hyenas fell to the ground with their tongues hanging out and their eyes rolling in their heads. Manny almost felt sorry for them when he looked at their thin, shrunken bodies. "Tell that to your buddies!" Manny declared as he sauntered off, leaving them in the dust. He went back to the wedding and was glad that it had been undisturbed.

Late into the evening, Kanodia and Moona thanked everyone and said good-bye, and went off alone to begin their life together.

Evana quietly followed them, hiding behind brush and trees. Finally, she just stood there, watching them run off under the stars. "One day," she whispered, "he'll be sorry he ever married that white wolf. He'll wish it were me!" She put her head down, but would not allow herself to cry. "Oh, Kanodia! How I have wanted you, thought of only you," she told herself. She shook her head. A mean, fierce look crept into her flashing green eyes. *Moona,* she thought, *you'll never be good enough for him! Never! One day, I'll make sure you know it!*

2
Never Good Enough

When Moona and Kanodia returned from their honeymoon, all their friends and family were there to welcome them home. The pack had been working for weeks on a big surprise for them. All the wolves wanted to be there when they showed them what they had made. They led the way, and Moona and Kanodia followed.

As they approached, they could see a cave all lit up in the night that was carved out of gigantic rock and looked like it led into a large hill. The hill itself actually seemed more like a small mountain. Manny stepped to the front and announced, "Kanodia and Moona, here is your new home, and we hope you like it!" They just stared in awe as they looked at it. Set around the outside of the cave were wooden stakes that stood six feet high and six feet apart. Intricately woven between each stake were thick heavy vines that were braided and tightly locked together to form a fence. The wolves had made sure that each stake was lit at the top so it illuminated the cave. They also created a special walkway that formed an aisle that led to the entrance. Alongside the walkway, they placed small boulders and mulched the aisle with plenty of dehydrated tree needles that softened each step.

On each side of the entranceway were lit torches, and directly above it was the magnificent scepter shining in all its glory.

The wolves had made a clearing around the front of the cave. There, they planted smaller exotic plants and wildflowers. Off to the right side, next to the cave, was a glorious waterfall. Just the right size, so you could play amidst the falls as the water-flow dropped gracefully into the deep blue quarry below.

Kanodia noticed that two strong vines were hung from a large tree that draped toward the water. This, he could see, allowed one to swing off the vine into the cool waters below.

"Oh!" cried Moona. "It's simply breathtaking!"

"Come on," Manny shouted, "there's more inside!"

As they approached the doorway they saw a covering of white netting. "This my friends, will keep the bugs away!" declared Manny.

"Where did you find that?" asked Kanodia.

"You know we all scout around, and men leave things in the forest all the time. And, well, if we can find a use for it, we do!" Manny answered proudly.

Inside, they had also made a huge stone hearth, and they already had a fire burning in it. Next to some of the plain stones, they could see that they had set enormous rare gems of white, green, blue and red, each gem dazzling in the firelight. A square hole was carved out of the wall and covered with sheer netting so they could see outside and look at the beautiful waterfall. On the slate floor, they had put several rugs of black mink that soothed and warmed each step they took.

Moona could not resist stretching out on the soft, black mink rug. Kanodia looked over at her. "Moona, you are a lovely sight," he said, marveling, as he had never seen her white fur look so luminescent as it did against the black mink. "Are you happy?" he asked.

"Beyond words. Why it is like a paradise, really. I don't know what to say, except how grateful and thankful I am with all of it, and especially all the good friends who did this for us." She smiled when she felt a soft, warm breeze blow into the cave. She inhaled deeply as the fragrance of white gardenia filled the air.

I agree with Moona," said Kanodia. "We are so impressed with all you have done and so very grateful!"

They all clapped as they shouted, "Welcome back!"

"Hey, what do you say we all go for a dip in the quarry?" asked Kanodia. They gave an excited *Rah!* and went running off toward the water. They each took turns swinging and jumping from the vines into the cool night waters, each wolf trying to outdo the other with their jumps and twirls from the vines. This went on for hours into the night and the wolves had never remembered having so much fun.

A day or two had passed and Kanodia decided he better find out all that had been happening since he had been away. He asked for a report from Manny and had found out that he had been diligent at keeping watch and there were no problems. Soon Kanodia had asked him to choose other wolves to be under his command. Again Manny was thrilled, and soon chose the strongest most trustworthy wolves to oversee smaller groups, as he could not be everywhere, Kanodia had pointed out to him.

Under their new leader's protection, all the wolves agreed, as time went by, that they had never lived so peacefully. Everyone had plenty and there were hardly ever any intruders trying to steal their food or go after the young ones. Should there be any attempt, the small army Kanodia had formed was quick as lightning to attack. Word of their strength quickly spread throughout the whole forest. Everyone seemed happy, and Kanodia had won their complete trust and respect. Meanwhile he and Moona lived in marital bliss.

"I never thought I could be this happy," Kanodia told Moona every morning when they woke.

"Somehow I knew that if I had you, I would be," she said, smiling up at him. "I've been thinking though, there is one thing I would like."

He looked at her surprised, "Anything you want!"

"A child!" she said excitedly. "I would love nothing more than to have your baby."

Kanodia's eyes lit up at the thought of it. "Me too," he agreed. "If my heart can hold another drop of joy, I would love a child."

Moona smiled at him, "I knew you would!" They both laughed as they dreamed together about what it would be like to have a baby of their own.

One after another, their friends were marrying too. Another year had passed, and Moona was beginning to get impatient. Kanodia reassured her that their baby would come. "Well, Evana and Manny married long after we did and she's expecting a baby very soon," she told him anxiously, not mentioning that Evana had been quick to brag about it to her.

Kanodia walked up to her and said, quietly, "I don't want you worrying. Our baby will come, you'll see," he said nuzzling her gently.

She smiled back at him. He always made her feel better.

Anyway, she thought to herself, *maybe Evana wasn't bragging, maybe she was just happy to be having a baby, after all she was married now and she and Manny seemed happy together.*

Yet another year passed and desperation began growing inside Moona's heart as one baby after another was born to each of her friends. Evana was now due to have her second one. She began to suspect that the others were whispering about her, as they'd abruptly stopped talking when they saw her approaching. Though she had no proof of it, she could sense it. Soon the old estrangement and feelings of being different again began to fill her mind. She thought she had left all that behind her so long ago. The ache from her childhood slowly began to return. Worse than even that, she felt she had failed her beloved husband.

One day Moona was on her way home from visiting with her parents. Suddenly, Evana and a couple of her friends headed her off. Moona stopped and looked at them questioningly.

"You still look as thin as ever, Moona," Evana said slyly.

Moona looked down for a second, self-conscious. Evana laughed. "I knew it, I knew you were a misfit from the first time I saw you. A white wolf!" she sneered. "Now it turns out you can't even give the leader of the pack a child!" Evana said as she chuckled an evil laugh. "See girls, I told you she was not good enough for Kanodia. Why he picked her, I'll never know!" The other two wolves nodded in agreement. "Well, Moona, it's too bad that you have to bring our leader to shame. Next time you see your reflection in that pretty quarry, remember, white wolves don't get to have babies! Nice try, Whitey," Evana said as she turned, "but I always knew you'd never be one of us. You'll never fit in!" Their laughing voices echoed eerily as they ran into the forest.

Moona was so shaken; she could feel her heart beating out of her chest. She felt unsteady and she couldn't seem to catch her breath. She thought she was either about to cry, or possibly scream. She ran off to hide from the others until she could gather her thoughts.

Later, when she had calmed a little, she went to sit by the quarry. She saw her reflection in the blue water. As she looked, she knew it was true. Deep down she had always known it; she was a misfit and would never be good enough for Kanodia. If Evana had beaten her with rocks, she couldn't have felt any more shattered. All the beauty, all the hope and love, everything was over. She would do what she must do for him, and the sooner the better, she decided.

Later that night, she found the courage to face Kanodia and tell him she was leaving him. She told him that he deserved so much more than she could give and that she had failed him. She had given up on the idea that she could ever have a child and would not listen to any more arguments or reassurances.

"It's too late. I want you to find yourself another wife, one that can give you the child you deserve."

"Never!" he cried, "I will never take another. My life has no meaning without you, whether we ever have children or not, can't you see that?" he pleaded.

She shook her head. "Please, stop," she said in a low, sad voice. "It's no use. Every time I look at you now I feel like a complete failure, and it has become unbearable for me to stay any longer." Kanodia pleaded with her for hours until he was out of words, and finally, exhausted, he fell asleep. The next morning when he awoke, she was gone.

After a week of searching he found her. She had retreated into a lonely, dark cave. He could not stand to see her like that, but, again, no matter what he said, she would not listen. She went further into the dark caves, telling him as she went that if he followed her or tried to see her again, she would leave again, promising him that he would not find her the next time.

Kanodia's heart broke into pieces.[2] He could actually feel something breaking inside. He was totally lost, and didn't have any idea of what he could do. He wandered through the forest alone. Days turned into weeks as he traveled, still further, into the thick dense woods through rain and cold, always feeling hungry and tired, not able to go back to the pack where he had lived with her in such happiness. Still, he could not escape the memories of her and the time they shared together. His life was now filled with sorrow and despair. He decided he would do anything to make her change her mind, and would not return to his home until he could think of a way to make her come back to him again.

---

[2] Brooks, Garth. "To Make You Feel My Love"

3
Calvin

Year 1896

If you asked the people who lived in the small, often chilly little town, where Calvin Bella grew up, what they thought of the young man, the first words out of their mouth would be *handsome* and then they'd say that *that was putting it mildly.* Then, they would tell you in a whisper that *he doesn't have a clue as to how good-looking he is, which makes him all the more attractive.* Tall and lean, with dark hair that's been streaked by the sun from all his work outside gathering materials for the next fine pieces of furniture he and his father would build, he had soft brown eyes and a quick smile, revealing perfectly white, straight teeth. The girls in town were always trying to find new ways of getting his attention, but he seemed to think of them all, only as friends.

Calvin's most vivid memory was when he had been only five. He remembered the day so clearly; it had been a brisk fall morning and his father had been at work. He and his mother walked into town to visit the local shops. They stopped to talk to people they knew, and gather the supplies she needed. As they walked toward home, his mother said to him, "I have a surprise for you." Smiling, she took a big multicolored lollipop out from behind her back while still balancing the heavy bag of items. She held it before her son.

Calvin was delighted. He had always stared at those luscious looking pops every time they went to town, and now he would have the pleasure of finally tasting it. He remembered thanking her many times, and she'd laugh, drawing him in close to her, calling him her "little treasure." He'd looked up at her, admiring her in her blue, wide-brimmed hat, her long dark hair tucked neatly underneath. Even though it was his mother, he'd thought even then that she was beautiful and he loved going places with her. They were together almost all of the time.

They were only about a mile or so from their home now, and suddenly the wind seemed to pick up intensely. They both stopped and looked up at the clouds that were closing in fast, dark and threatening. When they heard a huge crash of thunder, his mother had a frightened expression on her face and tightened her grip on his arm. Then a sharp spear of lightning looked like it was coming right toward them!

"Let's hurry! We must hurry and get home," she cried over the fierce winds, and they began to run.

The winds pushed against them now, and she set the bag down on the ground, leaving it and the lollipop behind. He didn't understand what was happening, but he saw the fright in her face. She seemed to be only concerned with holding onto him. As she picked him up, she covered her arms around him. He heard her saying something else, but could not make out the words, the winds whistling so loudly it carried every other sound away. Her hat was the first thing to be taken, and her hair fell loose, blowing in every direction. She fought to keep it out of her face. The wind screeched and thunder boomed while more and more bolts of lightning spears crashed toward the ground, almost like they were surrounding them.

Out of breath, they finally got to the top of a hill, and they spotted a small house in the distance. She had to put him down for a moment to rest. He watched her point to the little house, although he still couldn't hear her. He knew though that she was trying to get them out of the storm and to a safe place. As they pushed their way down the hill the wind pushed back harder. It was so strong that Calvin began to slip back almost feeling like he would be whisked away. She quickly picked him up again and fought her way down the hill while holding him tightly in her arms. Dirt and sand swirled around in the air, stinging their eyes. He could feel his mother struggling to push on. Fighting against the wind, like pushing back a tidal wave.

Just as they were about to head down the pebbled path that led to the little house, Calvin heard a loud thud, and his mother instantly fell to the ground, still holding him. Now, he wiggled his way out from under her, his own knees scraped and bleeding. He stared at her, not understanding what had happened. He knelt close to the ground beside her, but her eyes wouldn't open and she didn't move.

"Mum," he said, shaking her gently. "Please, Mum, open your eyes." He waited anxiously, but still she lay motionless.

As fast as the winds had come up is almost as quickly as they died down. Calvin spotted a well, and even at his young age he had known how to draw water. He ran to get some as fast as he could, and when he came back to her he knelt at her side. "Mum, drink some water," he said softly, hoping it would magically cure her. "Mum, please drink, please," he begged again, putting the little tin cup right next to her lips. Nothing. Finally, he dipped his finger in the cup and brought the moist droplets to her lips, spreading them around with his tiny finger. Still, she didn't move or utter a sound. He knew something was horribly wrong, and he was very frightened as feelings of dread crept into his young heart. He could think of nothing else to do.

Finally, he lay down beside her with tears streaming down his cheeks. Somewhere in his young heart he already knew that she was gone.[3] He slid closer to her, as close as he could get. He put his tiny hand on her now ashen face and stroked it gently. "Take me with you,

[3] Godspell. "By My Side"

Mum," he whispered through his tears. "Please, don't leave me here without you. Take me with you."

Calvin didn't remember what happened after that. He just knew that he would never see his mother again. A huge emptiness spread within him from that day on and would stay with him for many years to come, ever yearning to be filled.

His father was very sad and had explained as well as he could that God had taken her to heaven and that they would both see her again when their time came.

The next thing he knew was that he was standing with his father staring at what used to be their home. The storm had taken their house too, and left in its wake a pile of rubble. Almost everything they owned was destroyed or had blown away. His father found a picture of his mother buried beneath the rubble. He held it close to his heart almost as if he were holding her again, and it was still in its frame. He set it on a tree stump, probably somehow hoping it would make them feel like she was with them again.

Day after day, he watched while his father tried to rebuild a home for them, cutting down huge trees, chopping, fitting, and nailing. Some of the nearby neighbors tried to pitch in, but they had to rebuild or repair their own homes after the devastating storm. Finally, though, after months of living in a makeshift tent, the house was complete and much larger than the first one had been.

Calvin watched his father gather some large branches and pick up what he called his carving knife. He began to cut away at the bark, leaving a clean piece of wood. He then began to shape and carve as he held it up and announced to him, "This is going to be the first leg of our dining room set."

Calvin decided to try to find a branch of his own. Then he picked up a small knife, sat down beside him and began to whittle away to make the second leg. Calvin saw his father watching him, even though he didn't look straight at him. His father didn't say anything, and he even thought he saw, for the first time in months, a small smile cross his lips.

He and his father had, in time, furnished the entire house with all handmade furniture that they had carved, sanded, and created themselves. They received so many compliments on their wood-working, that it was actually what had given his father the idea to start his own fine furniture business.

About a year later, Calvin's father came to him saying they needed to talk. He explained that he had met a woman that he wanted to marry. "She's a good, hard-working woman, and you need someone to care for you."

Calvin was shocked, he thought they were doing okay by themselves, but his father said that a boy needs a mother. "Really, Calvin, it will be fine," he said, trying to reassure him. He paused at the door. "No one can ever take your mother's place, for me or for you, but we have to go on son," he said gently, and then he left the room.

A candle burned on a small table that was placed under the window in his room. He heard the door close downstairs and he looked out his window. Rain beat against the windowpane, but he could still see her. She held a dark colored parasol and wore a darker colored cape. The fog rolled in and it was like she was walking in a gray mist. He watched his father carry a lantern and help her get into the back of a covered coach. Yet, even from a distance, Calvin could feel the coldness between them. *That's it?* he thought, *He just walks in here and changes my whole life again. Why can't things stay the same?*

A month later they were married and Alice became his stepmother. *"What should I call you, Ma'am?"* He asked her meekly.

"Ma'am will be fine," she answered simply, and that was the end of their first conversation.

Calvin had seen that his father had been right; she was a hard worker. She cooked and cleaned and saw to it that he had what he needed. She was always busy, and even when she sat in the parlor, she'd be knitting or sewing. He also noticed that she hardly ever smiled. Calvin tried his best to be kind to her, but she remained aloof.

Once, when he was still very young, he had been quite ill, and she'd sat with him and put cool cloths on his head to bring his fever down, fed him soup, and tended to him until he was well. He had tried to hug her and thank her, but she remained stiff, not returning his embrace. He remembered feeling embarrassed and hurt, vowing to himself never to do that again. He remained respectful toward her, but she never changed her demeanor, and he decided to just try to stay out of her way.

His father, in the meantime, worked very long days in the workshop he had added to the house. Orders for his furnishings were endless, and soon he was known to be the finest of craftsman. He hired on another man named Emmett, and Calvin would watch for hours learning all he could about making fine furniture.

About a year or so after his father married, his stepmother announced she was having a baby. Calvin had never seen her look so happy. That is, until her baby, who turned out to be babies, were born. She smiled all the time with her twin boys and showered them with all the affection and attention that Calvin thought she didn't even have within her to give. They were all happy with the boys, Liam and Lance. They filled the house with life, and he was determined to be a good brother to them.

As the babies grew, Calvin would spend time with the boys, but he noticed that she was always peering in on them, a look of disapproval on her face. When they were old enough to play ball, he was the first to try to teach them, making them each a fine bat of their own. He would begin to play with them, and just when he thought they were enjoying it, she would give one of her looks and they would tell him that they didn't want to play anymore. He'd watch them run off, leaving him bewildered. He made them sleighs for the snow and he'd buy them toys when he went to town, and still they would act just like her. *Aloof* is how he thought of it. He was baffled with all of them. This went on for years, until finally he, sadly, just gave up trying.

As he got older, Calvin became more and more a part of the furniture business. Now he was able to do all parts of the job. His father was very happy about it and told him at least once a week that the business would be all his one day. What he didn't know how to tell his father was that he didn't want to make furniture for the rest of his life, at least not until he had gotten the chance to travel and see some of the world. He wasn't sure exactly where he wanted to go yet. One place that intrigued him most was a faraway place called Morningstar Mountain. He had heard that it was supposed to be one of the most beautiful places in the world. He also heard talk that there were hidden diamond mines there that had yet to be found. The thought of traveling to a place like that and looking for the treasure thrilled him. He had mentioned it to his father on a couple of occasions, but his father insisted that it was simply all rumors. A yearning to go and find out for himself grew stronger each day. He knew he could never tell him that, since his mother had died, this place had never felt like home to him again. Somewhere in his heart, he knew he didn't belong here, but he wanted to please his father too.

Every Sunday they were all required to go to church. Each time he went, they sang the same songs, gave the same announcements and recited the same prayers. He felt there had to be more to it than just going to church. "If you want to go to Heaven, you must go to church, be a good person and give to the poor. This is what God expects from us," his stepmother told them firmly.

He decided to find out for himself. He decided to read the bible, and he was surprised to find out that God wants us to know Him, and He knows all about us. God, who is creator of all things, wants to be our friend. So, he began talking with God in his thoughts, telling him everything. Somehow he knew without a doubt that He was listening.

One day he was walking home from town and he took the same route he and his mother had traveled so long ago on that tragic day. The memories of his young mother filled his mind again; she was always telling him stories and singing him sweet hymns that lulled him to sleep each night.

He sat down on the hill. As he thought of the memories of that day, a gentle, warm breeze softly blew by him. In that moment, he could feel his mother's essence, as if she were there with him for a second. Just then, appearing out of nowhere, a soft, white, perfect feather rolled up onto his lap.

Calvin sat there holding the delicate feather, staring at it, not moving, feeling elated, but also shocked. Wow," he breathed out loud. It was enough for him. Calvin felt like it was a gift given to him from above. It seemed like a reassurance that his mother was okay, peaceful, safe. He had felt it when that warm breeze had blown past him, and he knew someday they would be together again. At that moment, the wound in his heart began to heal a little. He felt something warm instead of the emptiness that had been there since his mother had been gone.

Now that he was finished with school, and had graduated. He filled his days with work and he would go into town with a few friends on the weekends.

Sometimes, his father would send him out to deliver the furniture. One day he was to deliver a table and chairs to a woman. "Her name is Mrs. Tag," his father had told him. "I think her first name is Janice, if I remember right. She's a kind woman," he went on as he and Calvin carried the pieces to the wagon. "She's been widowed for many years. You've probably seen her at church. Very devoted to the church, I recall," he said as he passed the last chair to Calvin.

Calvin secured the last few pieces with rope and made sure they would not fall off. "Okay," he said to his father, "I'm off!" His father watched him pull away.

He found the yellow house with ease and realized he must have passed by it many times before. The house had a friendly charm, and the woman was standing in the doorway smiling as he pulled up. She waved toward him, beckoning him inside. She was a small, petite woman with blonde hair that she wore piled gracefully on her head. He noticed right away that she was very friendly and kind. Maybe he saw it in her crystal-clear blue eyes that seemed to have a warm smile hidden within. Calvin thought he might have seen her before, but could not remember exactly when or where. He liked her instantly, and followed as she showed him around her home. Then he carefully brought in each piece of furniture and placed it exactly where she wanted it to go.

"Now," she said as she ran her hand across the smooth wooden table, "have you ever in all your life seen a piece of wood shine so brightly?" Calvin chuckled at her enthusiasm and noticed she had a very slight southern accent. "Now what kind of a dumb thing is that for me to say? Of course you have. You must see wood gleam like that every day," she said, laughing. "Well, bless your heart for bringin' this over to me," she stared again, admiring the furniture. "I'm gonna keep this set gleaming like glass."

"I'm glad you like it," he said cheerfully, not telling her that he had made the set.

"Like it," she exclaimed joyfully, "why, this is a real blessing you've brought me, and so are you! I could tell right away!" She laughed and stared at her new furniture.

Calvin felt good knowing it made her so happy. She offered him a piece of blueberry pie that she had just baked. He could smell the delicious aroma in the air. After hesitating a moment, she insisted, and he agreed.

She asked him a few questions about his job and his family, and he answered in between bites of her fabulous pie. She told him she had lost her husband many years ago, but added that she had one son who worked way down south for his wife's family. She went to visit now and again, and they'd come up to see her and stay at the house, but it wasn't often enough. "That's why I keep the house, I guess. It has so many memories, and my son just loves to be able to come home now and again," she said happily. "The problem with this old house, though, is that it needs a lot of minor repairs. Say, you wouldn't happen to know anyone who wants to make a little extra money doing some repairs, would you?" Calvin told her he'd be happy to help out and told her as he left he would stop by soon to do the work.

By the end of the week, he had decided to go back to Mrs. Tag's and help her. She was delighted to see him. He began by tightening the loose hinges on her doors. Then, he started to re-string some of the old windows. After a few hours of work, he stayed on and talked with her for a while.

He began to visit the nice woman quite often and they soon became good friends. One day when he had finished patching the roof, she started to tell him about a few of the adventures she'd had with her husband. She said that the best trip was to Morningstar Mountain.

Calvin's eyes widened. "You mean you've been to Morningstar?"

"Oh, yes, and what a place it is. Why, there is no place like it on the whole earth!" As she spoke, he noticed she had a faraway look in her eyes. Calvin wanted to hear every detail. "Well, it began a few years after we were married. Anyway, my husband had heard of the beauty of Morningstar, but I'll tell you I think he was most intrigued when he heard people talking about the hidden diamond mines. Being the adventurer that he was, well, that was it; he had his mind all made up before I could say a word. Actually, though, I was very excited, myself, to see this wondrous place we had heard so much about. So, we made our plans and set out for the journey. It was a long, hard journey back then, and we got lost a few times trying to find the hidden land, but eventually we got there. The mountain itself is huge, and when the sun rises, why, Calvin, you just can't believe your eyes. It starts very slowly at dawn, and when the sun comes up behind the mountain, as soon as it reaches its highest peak, the sun bursts out its rays, reaching out and forming a star with all the colors of the rainbow. It is truly magical!"

Calvin was totally immersed in her story, and tried to picture it in his mind as she went on.

"At the foot of the mountain is Morningstar Village, and it is like another world. I was so mesmerized by the lush beauty. It's simply beyond words." She stopped as if to look for words to describe what she had seen, but shook her head and they both laughed. "Well, we managed to find a small inn to stay at when we got there, figuring that when we were settled we'd find a place of our own. It seemed that, no sooner had we arrived than I found out we were going to have our first child. My husband was thrilled and began to look for work there, but there just wasn't any to be found. So, he set out to find the diamond mines. Many people in the town did try to talk him out of going out alone to search for the mine. They warned him, telling him others had tried and failed, and some had never returned again! However, he would not be stopped. He told me to stay put, not to worry, and that he would return as soon as he found the diamonds. Weeks went by and I didn't hear a word, and eventually I was simply frantic with worry! I began alerting people in the town to let them know he was missing." She went on, remembering sadly now. "Finally, one day, two men came to the door and told me that he had been killed. They said that wild animals had gotten to him, and that they were very sorry. My first thought was that he would never see his child, who turned out to be a boy, a wonderful son, and he would have been so proud of him," she stopped and dabbed away her tears.

"I'm so sorry," he said sympathetically.

She shook her head, "No, I'm sorry. I always cry when I talk about it." She took a few moments and, after calming, she went on. "Well, anyway, I was almost completely out of money. I knew I needed to leave and go back home to my family. Somehow, I found my way back. I lived with my parents here in this house, and they helped me raise my boy. They are both gone now, and I do miss each one of them dearly, especially my husband, who was so young when I lost him. Oh, what might have been? For a long time, I regretted going to Morningstar, but it was the most beautiful place I have ever seen!" Her eyes lit up again with the memory of it. "We probably should have heeded what we were told by the people in the town, but it shouldn't stop anyone from seeing it, and if you ever get the opportunity, you should go!"

"I wish I could," he said, "but my father insists it's all rumors." Calvin paused and looked away. "Well, I better get back to work. Thank you for telling me. Just hearing about it makes me want to go even more, and now I know it really exists."

"Oh, it's true, alright," she thought for a minute and asked him to wait. She went into the other room and came back a moment later and said, "Calvin, I want you to have this."

She handed him a colorful stone that sparkled like glass. It was layered, and each layer appeared to be made of a different jewel. She smiled. "It's from the Village, and the next time someone tells you it's all rumors, show them this."

His eyes lit up as he examined it. He had never seen anything like it before. "It's beautiful," he paused as he looked over the stone again, "I've somehow got to see this place. I've got to find it, but how, where?"

She was glad to see him so enthusiastic. “Well, you travel to the very edge of the west, and from there you can sail, or maybe even fly in those balloons people talk about now, it’s up to you. When you start to see land and mountains, follow the mountain peaks at dawn. When the sun rises, one mountain will form a starburst and shine with all the colors of the rainbow. That is Morningstar Mountain, and the Village is at the foot of that mountain.”

“Thank you again for sharing your story with me, and for the fantastic stone! This really means a lot to me, Mrs. Tag. I meant what I said. I really want to go there and I am going to try to find a way.”

She nodded her head, “When the time is right, the good Lord will find a way and you’ll get there, Calvin. I really believe you are meant to go. I don’t know why, but something tells me you are definitely meant to go there.”

Calvin felt like his heart had dropped in his chest as she spoke those words; it was the first time he heard someone say what he had been feeling for so long. “You have no idea how much it means to me to hear you say that.”

She smiled at him warmly and looked him right in the eye, “Oh, I think I do. Sometimes people spend a lifetime in a place they don’t belong because they won’t follow their heart. You can see it in their eyes if you really look.”

When Calvin slept that night he had a dream. He saw a girl, but could not see her face. She wore a flowered wreath in her long, dark hair. He thought she was calling his name, her voice as pretty as a song. She was waving her hand behind her, summoning him to follow. He reached out to her, but she was gone.

The next day when he woke, he decided that he would tell his father about his plans to go to Morningstar Mountain. He spent the entire morning working in the shop, nervous about confronting his father. It was Emmett's day off, and he was grateful to talk to his father alone. When he sat down in the kitchen to eat lunch, Calvin approached him.

"Father." He looked up, and Calvin set the jeweled stone down gently on the table. His father looked at him, puzzled.[4]

"It's not a rumor," he said. "Morningstar Mountain is real, and Mrs. Tag gave me this stone to prove it."

He stared at the rock for a moment and then put down his fork. "Son, listen, I know you want to travel and see the world, and you can after you've established yourself. It's time maybe for you to think about finding yourself a wife. We'll get you a home of your own, and you and your bride can take trips together. You'll have a house, a wife and of course you'll have the furniture business."

"Father, whoever it is I am going to marry, she is not here in this town," Calvin said as he studied his face for

[4] Stevens, Cat. "Father and Son"

a long moment. "You think you'll never see me again, don't you?" His voice grew quiet at the thought. "But," he paused again, "you will," he answered quietly.

His father just stared at him. Calvin quickly tried to change the subject and went on to describe the mountain as Mrs. Tag had told him.

His father shook his head. "Could you really, in all honesty, promise me that you would ever come back here to live?"

Calvin paused a moment and began to answer and then stopped. Shaking his head, he looked down. "I couldn't promise. I don't know what would happen," he said sadly.

His father got up from the chair and went over to the window, his back toward his son. He stared out for a long time as Calvin watched him. Then he spoke, and Calvin had never heard his father's voice sound so broken and sad, as if he were trying to stop himself from sobbing. "Calvin, please, I want so much for you to be happy, anything I could do," he choked back his sobs as he turned around to face him. "I know I have no right to say this because it's your life, but I can't bear to lose you, Calvin. I really just can't take another loss." He stepped closer toward him, his voice becoming a whisper. "You are all I have left of your mother. To me, it would be like losing her all over again." Then he embraced him for a long time.

Calvin was speechless. He realized that his father had never gotten over the loss of his mother, and that neither one of them ever would. He understood now how his father felt, and he was angry with himself for putting him through this anguish. He looked at him reassuringly and said, "I miss her too. You were right, it was just a stupid idea. Don't give it another thought. I'm not going anywhere."

From that day on, Calvin worked in the shop side by side with his father and Emmett. Never again did he even utter a word about leaving, no matter how much he wanted to travel. He would not ever see his father upset like that again. Not as long as he had anything to do with it.

4
Time to Say Goodbye

The next time Calvin went to visit Mrs. Tag, he told her what had happened between him and his father.

"You are such a good son," she said, "your father must be so proud. I sure enough know your mother would have been!"

He smiled at her warmly. They talked a while, but before he left he said, "By the way, do you still go to our church? My father told me he thought he had seen you there."

"That dry bones church!" She exclaimed, "I haven't gone there in two or three years." Calvin couldn't help laughing at the way she described it. "Now don't get the wrong idea, it's just that they seem to do the same thing each week, and that's good, I guess, but for me, I like a church that's alive! I go to the little church over on Pleasant Street. They really got the spirit there! You should come on over some Sunday and see if it suits you."

"Maybe I will," he said as he went on his way.

The next Sunday he did go to the little church on Pleasant Street, and he could see why Mrs. Tag liked it so well. So did he. They sang a new song and he had loved it. As the Reverend Cressel spoke, Calvin listened closely.[5]

"Why do such bad things happen if God loves us so much? That seems to be the big question people ask me," the Reverend announced in a kind, strong voice. "The truth is God doesn't make bad things happen! There are evil forces in this world. We are not in heaven yet. God loves us all so much that he gave His only begotten son, who gave His life for us, that whoever believes in Him will not die, but will live on in heaven forever." he went on.

"God has a perfect plan for our lives and a perfect time for everything. Sometimes the terrible things that happen to us give us the strength and the character we need to fulfill the plan He has for us. He says that His thoughts are different from our thoughts. He tells us there is a time to laugh and a time to cry, a time to plant and a time to harvest, a time for war and a time for peace, a time to be born and a time to die." he nodded.

"Everything happens for some reason. God is not always behind that reason, though. There are thousands of reasons, and we cannot understand them all. What we can understand though is God's promise to us, which is if we love Him and trust Him, He will make all things, no matter how bad they may seem, turn around and work for good for His people." he smiled.

---

[5] Greenbaum, Norman. "Spirit In The Sky"

"So I ask the congregation to wait on the Lord and look for Him because He works in mysterious ways."

Calvin thought of the soft white feather as the minister went on.

"If you look for Him sincerely, the bible says He will let you find Him. Trust in Him and He will make a way for you where you thought there was no way. He will take the bad and turn it for good. These are His promises to His people. We can walk in peace knowing that He is with us through all things. Peace comes from understanding that we are far more than flesh and blood. That we are spirit and your spirit will never die. If we live believing in Him, even though our bodies should die, we will find ourselves in Heaven where there is no more sorrow or tears and we will live on with him forever."

Calvin wanted to know what he was meant to do, to find his purpose. He had to find out God's plan for his life.

It had been a couple of years since Calvin had vowed he would not leave. Since then, he had kept busy with work and even dated a couple of girls in town, immediately knowing that they were not right for him. Now he began to wonder if he really would be able to keep that promise. It seemed that he spent most of his time trying to push thoughts of leaving out of his mind. Then, even at night in his dreams, the girl would come to him, calling. He tried to hide his feelings from his father, but inside he was growing more dissatisfied by the day.

It was like his own mind was becoming a battlefield, torn between his desires to travel and with his loyalty to his father. He began to go out jogging at night; it seemed to relieve the pressure in some ways. One evening, after a long run, he decided to start writing his thoughts down in a journal. Some nights he just rambled on about what was happening on that particular day. Other times, though, he wrote of his deepest wishes and feelings. This helped to clear his mind. One night he wrote about his dream:

At night the paradise it calls,
It lets me glimpse beyond its walls.
I dream of it now, both night and day,
I spend my time trying to wish it away.

Her sweet voice, it calls, "come here,"
Never her face, though I'd know her anywhere.
I've tried to find her in dreams so long,
Yet when I reach out, she's always gone.

Why are you calling, see what you do?
My heart is torn between here and you!
I ask myself what is right for me,
And it's there with you I want to be.

"Hold on," I say it every day,
I know someday there will be a way.
Don't pull on my heartstrings any more,
Let me go for now, and close that door.

I look toward Heaven and I feel
It's not just a dream; it's all quite real.
The land it waits so patiently,
The girl who hides her face, I'll see.

I cannot hurt a good man so strong,
For he believes this is where I belong.
Though I know you are my destiny,
My dream remains nothing more for me...

The days drawled on and turned into weeks that turned into months. Then another year had passed. He still managed to act happy around his father, and he was glad to see that his father was content.

He still visited Mrs. Tag and went to church. It was after a service at the church that he decided that he was being totally selfish. When he told Mrs. Tag, she agreed, then she laughed and said, "Bless your heart Calvin, I'm just foolin' with you. The truth is you are feeling exactly the way you're supposed to feel. God has a plan for you and He has given you the desire to go after that plan. However, trust Him that there is a reason for you to be here right now. Show him that you trust Him and thank Him right where you are in your life now. When the time comes, and it will, the doors of change will open, and you will be free to go with your father's blessing and the good Lord's blessing, above all!"

"You know, you always know just what to say," he told her warmly. "You, Mrs. Tag, have been a true friend and a great blessing to me!"

He began to be more thankful for the good things he had and he realized that he was a pretty blessed guy. After all, so many people had far more things to worry about than he did, and he owed so much to his father for the good and prosperous life he had given them. He began to spend more of his time off with his father, and they took walks and laughed together and he found that he loved spending time with him. He realized what a great father he had.

Other times he decided to look around and help out some older people in the town that were not able to get around on their own. He began to make furniture pieces for the church to give to some needy people. Then he found out some elderly people, Chester and Elsie Jewell, who lived not far from him, needed someone who could go into town for them. He picked up their groceries and brought them in for them. From time to time he would make some repairs to their home too. Chester told him of his battles in the civil war, and Calvin found his stories to be dangerous, tragically sad, and very heroic. He enjoyed Mrs. Jewell with her whimsical hats that she had decorated with flowers and birds. She found joy in the smallest of things, and Calvin learned a great deal from her about being happy. He often found that those that he helped ended up helping him in ways he really didn't understand, but he was very grateful for the people he had gotten to know, and more content.

It was late that year that many people in town were becoming very ill. The sickness would come on suddenly, and, then, in a matter of days, it would either worsen from complications, or begin to ease. They called it influenza, and the townspeople were more than worried. It was spreading among them so quickly, it was all anyone talked about. No one knew how you got it or what to do about it.

Suddenly, without any warning signs, Calvin's father took to his bed. The doctor was called in immediately, and the family was told it was influenza.

Calvin sat by his father's bedside day and night, praying he would recover, fearing all the while that he would not. He seemed to be growing worse and frailer by the day. The doctor was called again a few days later and told the family pneumonia had set in and it didn't look good.

One evening, deep into the wee hours of the night, Calvin woke hearing his father weakly calling for him. *He is so very weak,* Calvin thought, with panic rising inside. Calvin stared at him, stunned for a moment at seeing his strong father suddenly look so frail. It took all his father's strength to motion for him to come closer. Calvin dashed to his bedside and leaned over to listen. His father's words were faint and he gasped for air in between sentences.

"Son, I want you to know how happy you've made me and how proud, greatly proud I am of you," he stopped briefly. "I think, though, that I may have done wrong by you in asking you to stay here. It was selfish of me. I hope you will forgive me." Calvin immediately began to reassure him, but his father held up his hand to stop him. He knew it was taking all his strength just to speak, so he was quiet. "I never got over losing your mother. I loved her more than life itself. That is why I am not sad to be leaving this world, knowing I'll finally be with her again."

Calvin was in full panic now. "Father, please don't talk like that, you're not going anywhere," he exclaimed with a huge ache forming in his throat.

"I want," he was fighting for breath, "I want you to go and do all the things you have longed to do. I know you stayed for me, and I could not have asked for a better son. You have blessed me, and now I want to give you my blessing as I say good-bye. I love you, my son. Go and be happy, be blessed, and may God give you all your heart's desires."

Calvin could not speak, his throat throbbing and aching. He was totally overcome with grief and loss and he could do nothing but put his head in his hands and weep at his father's bedside.

That night his father fell into a coma. By mid-morning his spirit had flown away to join his mother.

Calvin was deeply grieved; his only comfort during that gray, dark time was that he knew that his father and his mother would be together again, at last. He went through the next six months in a thick fog. He would be forever grateful that he had been with his father in his final years.

Calvin began to realize that now having both his parents gone, there really was no more reason to stay. He spent the next few months trying to put everything in order so his stepmother and the boys would be well taken care of. In his father's will, he left the business solely to Calvin, as well as half of everything else he owned. The other half went to his stepmother.

Calvin hired two very capable men to work with Emmet to keep the business going. Emmet, of course, would be left in charge of the business. He trusted Emmet, who had been a very honest and loyal worker over the years. He also knew that he would see to it that the quality of the workmanship was maintained.

He only had to tell Mrs. Tag, and then he would talk to his stepmother. He decided to go see Mrs. Tag first, and of course she was thrilled for him. "Oh, I know you're going to be just fine Calvin," she said and clapped her hands together and leaned back in the big chair she always liked to sit on.

"I promise I'll let you know as soon as I get there. I will write to you."

"I'll be lookin' for that letter," she smiled, though her eyes seemed to be filling with tears.

"Hold on a minute, I have a surprise for you," he announced as he went back out to get the surprise. He carried it in two pieces. It was a hutch to match her dining set. It had drawers on the bottom piece for her to keep things in, and shelves on the top for her to display her pretty china pieces. He quickly set it up for her as she watched with a delighted look on her face.

"I hope you like it," he said after he had arranged it for her. She went on and on at how lovely it was and how well it fit, and she was amazed that it matched her dining set so perfectly.

"Really, you did not have to do this! I was so happy just to have had your friendship."

He wanted to tell her how much she had meant to him over the years, that she'd been like a second mother to him, but the right words just wouldn't come.

They talked on a little while, and he was sorry to leave her, but he knew she was happy for him. She told him that she believed it was God's plan for him. As he walked out her front door for what he thought might be the last time, he turned back to her and said, "I hope, I mean, I just want—"

She touched his shoulder then and nodded her head. "I know, Calvin," she said gently with a tear in her eye, "and I feel the same way."

The time had come for him to talk to his stepmother. Though he would have put it off forever, it was getting closer to leaving and he knew he had to face her. He wanted to make sure that she and the boys would not have any financial worries when he was gone. After dinner, he found her sitting in the parlor, knitting. She sat erect in her high-collared, long, gray dress that she wore so often. He had put the moment off as long as he could, but he would be leaving the following morning, so it was now or never. He cleared his throat as he entered the parlor. "Good evening, ma'am. Do you have a few minutes? I'd like to talk to you."

She barely looked at him and motioned to the chair across from her, and as he sat he leaned forward, feeling very uneasy.

"I will be leaving in the morning before you rise up," he paused briefly waiting for her to look up from her knitting. He noticed silver threads running through her hair and he was surprised that he hadn't seen them before. Finally, to break the awkward silence, she bobbed her head up momentarily, giving him a puzzled look, but said nothing and went back to her knitting.

"Well," he went on, "you've heard me talking to the boys about traveling. I've mentioned it at dinner several times, and I am sure you must have heard me even though you did not say anything." He stopped for a moment to see if she would say something now. Silence. "Anyway," he cleared his throat, "as you know, Father stated in his will that he had left the business to me, as well as half of his money and half of this house and, as you know, the other half is to be yours."

She continued to knit.

He swallowed and said, "I… I have managed to save some money, and I've decided to turn the house and the business over to you and the boys. All I wish to take is his carving knife and a few pictures."

She smiled, shaking her head, and let out a small sarcastic laugh. Still, without even looking at him, she covered her mouth as if she were concealing some secret.

Now he was really confused. "What is it that you find funny?" he asked, having no idea what to make of her strange reaction. She shook her head quickly and continued to ignore him. Calvin leaned back and pondered a moment. "No," he said more persistently, "I need to know, why the grin, why the laugh?"

Again she shook her head, still concealing a half smile. "It's nothing, really."

He pressed on, "It's just that I thought you would be happy to receive the house and the business. I guess I just didn't expect you to not say anything, especially after all these years. I thought you might care that I am leaving here, and I am really surprised you would just start laughing. So tell me, please, I need to know what is so funny?" Clearly becoming annoyed with his persistence, she pushed her knitting down on her lap firmly and looked up. Calvin waited and she just stared at him, but he still wanted an answer. "Well?" he asked.

"I just think you've made a foolish decision," she snapped.

At first, his mouth dropped and he caught himself. This was hardly the reaction he had expected. He swallowed and finally asked, slowly, "Why is it foolish?"

She shook her head again as if he should know the answer. "Here you are, leaving your home in which you've been given everything to go who knows where, traipsing across the country, chasing rainbows or whatever. And what do you do, give every bit of security you have away. Don't misunderstand me, the boys and I are happy to have it," she paused, "but it just struck me funny." She raised her brows and tightened her lips. Before she resumed her knitting, she stopped and quickly pressed two fingers to her lips as if to keep her from laughing at him again.

He found himself staring at her again for a long moment, and then he got up to walk out of the room. Then, he stopped himself at the threshold. Turning back to face her, he said, "What has this all been about, anyway?"

Still knitting, she gave a sigh of annoyance and refused to look at him. His voice became shaky. He felt like his heart was beating wildly, but he began to question her more forcefully. "What has this all been about?" he repeated. "I need to understand. I mean, why marry my father? Why bring up his son? Why? Why did you do it?" he folded his arms and waited, determined to get to the truth.

"It was part of the arrangement," she said through gritted teeth. "I wanted to marry and have a home and a family of my own. Your father had said he needed a wife that would care for you and tend to your needs, and as far as I am concerned, I have done so!"

Calvin nodded and began to understand her for the first time since they had met on that rainy, gray night. "A job," he said sadly, shaking his head. "I guess I was just a job to you, so you could get what you wanted."

She slammed down her knitting on her lap. "I want you to stop this questioning right now!" she demanded.

A pain shot threw his heart like a dagger as he looked at her now with her tightly woven hair, her sharp direct features, and heard her callous words. It was as if a veil had been lifted. All that he had felt over the years became clear, her detachment and her lack of any attention toward him or affection. She never even asked him a question about his life. Never did she make any attempt whatsoever to even get to know him. She even seemed to turn the twins away from him. She wouldn't even give him that much of a chance. "He could have hired someone to do the *work* that you've done."

She glared at him now. "I did what your father expected me to do. Do you think I should have poured my heart into another woman's child? Why would I, so you could grow up and stand before me like you're doing now and tell me I could never measure up to your mother? Do you think I am so foolish as to even put myself in a position like that?" She didn't wait for his answer. "One thing you should have learned about me is that I am no fool!"

As she spoke memories came flooding back of his mother, her soft eyes, her gentle touch and her warm reassuring words that were always filled with love. *Oh, God,* he thought, *how I miss her.* A lump grew in his throat, but he swallowed it away. He did not want her to see him like that. "And the boys?" he asked hoarsely. "You taught my own brothers to keep me at a distance, didn't you?"

She looked straight at him, still unmovable, her eyes showing no emotion, always unwavering in all her decisions.

"Had you let my brothers and I get to know each other, I may have believed your reasons for being the way you have been toward me. But now I see it was simply just cold, and forgive me if I'm wrong, but to me it was not only cold, but bitter and mean." He bit his bottom lip to keep it from trembling, not from fear, but from the pointless grief and loss. "Well, you can consider my share of the house and the business that I have given you as payment in full."

He tried to sleep that night, but he felt more than ever like a stranger in his own home. He looked in on the twins for the last time and then closed the door. He knew now, when he left the house he had grown up in, that he would not even be missed.

At the break of dawn, still feeling exhausted, he boarded the train. He vaguely heard the conductor as he shouted, "All aboard!" Calvin found a window seat and was startled when he heard the whistle scream its last warning that the train was departing. He never thought he would feel this bad when the day arrived for him to pursue his lifelong dream. Yet, it seemed that all he could think about were all the years of his life leading up to this point. It was like his last conversation with his stepmother had unleashed an ocean of mixed feelings inside him. Things just kept rolling over and over in his mind and he could not stop it.

She had thought of him as a fool. He knew that now. Well, maybe he was, but did she know the future? He remembered it all as the train began to move faster on the tracks.[6] It was as if he were seeing his past rolling through his mind in a rush, like the wheels on the train. He ran his hands through his hair as the memories flooded him.

That last night, trying to say goodbye, thinking he was doing the very best he could for her and the twins before he left... *Was it him?* He wondered. *Was it just him she didn't like?* He kept seeing her as she sarcastically laughed at him for believing that he needed to try to begin a new life somewhere else.

He remembered the first time he had seen her out his window on that rainy, cold night. He pictured it in his mind again, the candle that burned on the little table under the windowpane. It had been like she had stepped out of the fog. Then another scene flashed through his mind, when he had been ill and he had hugged her and

---

6 Electric Light Orchestra. "Big Wheels"

she had not returned his embrace. All those years trying to please her, trying desperately to befriend his own brothers. But it was never good enough to ever get any of them to what, even like him?

This was no longer his home, nor would it ever be again. He had no place to go back to, even if he wanted to. Now that both his parents were gone, he knew he would have to start over, looking to find a place to call home.

All that was left were the memories and the two gray stones that lay side by side that bore his parent's names.

6
Up, Up, and Away

After riding on the train for two days, he was happy to hear the conductor call out that this was the last stop.

As he stepped off the train, he looked around. The old town looked a lot like any other, though he noticed the roads were more dusty and worn. There was a General store, a saloon, a barbershop, and, in the center of it all, a small diner. He pulled out an advertisement from a magazine that he had saved that featured an ad about air balloon flying in Netstown.

He walked into the town square and it was still early morning. He went into the diner and asked some people who were eating breakfast if they knew how he could get to Netstown. A scraggly man with a missing front tooth said he could give him a ride right to it, if the price was right. He said his name was Whippett, and he spoke with a slow drawl.

Calvin couldn't help staring for a moment; he had never seen a man with such a long neck and a huge Adam's apple. Calvin sat down and they agreed on a price, and Whippett promised he could get him there quickly.

Whippett said he would be ready in a flash. Calvin watched him as he dipped his bread into his runny egg yolk and slapped it in his mouth. While he was still sloshing the food around, he said, "Follow me, partner." He rose up and put on a screwy looking hat, something like a cowboy would wear, except it was mashed down at the top.

Calvin was staring at him, then caught himself as Whippett turned back to look at him. Calvin smiled. *What am I getting myself into*, he thought. As he followed him out, he saw Whippett pull up his pants that were falling down as he walked, revealing a small crack.

"Well, this is my get up," said Whippett proudly.

Calvin looked at the rig. He could see that he would have to ride in the back. He didn't have much choice in the matter and decided as long as it got him where he wanted to go, he would make do with it. It had one horse and just enough room for the driver. The driver's seat lifted up, and Calvin was able to put his backpack and duffel bag inside.

Whippett held out his hand for payment, and Calvin got out his money.

"Climb aboard!" Whippett yelled as he shoved the cash into his pocket.

Calvin got in the wagon, and no sooner did he sit down than they took off.[7]

The horse began running faster and faster through the narrow trails in the woods. He was bumping up and down. Each time he took a corner, Calvin would slide to

[7] ZZtop. "LaGrange"

the other side of the wagon. He was holding on for dear life. Barely keeping his grip, he yelled to Whippett to slow down, but Whippett could not hear him over the galloping of the horse with the wind in his ears.

Calvin rode like that for hours, twisting and turning down narrow paths. The wagon was so small, all he could do was try to hold on. Suddenly, they hit a huge hole and *bang!* The wooden wheels slammed underneath him, and Calvin flew into the air and crashed back down. Before he could grab hold again, they hit another hole. *Bang!* Calvin flew up in the air and out of the wagon, this time, crashing to the ground. He quickly got up and ran after him, but Whippett was gone in the dust with all his belongings and his money.

Calvin ached from head to toe. He was so dizzy, he leaned up against a tree and threw up. He had barely started his journey and he was already sick and broke. "What am I going to do now?" he yelled to no one. He brushed himself off and began walking. All he could do was try to follow the trail of dust.

After hours of walking, he was tired and thirsty. He stepped off the path when he saw a small babbling brook. He drank the water as fast as he could. He found a small clearing under a tree and he piled up some leaves making a cushion. He lay down on it to rest and, within minutes, he fell asleep.

The next morning Calvin thought he heard someone talking, and when he opened his eyes, there, staring at him in the face, was a large frog.

“Ah!” he yelled, and the frog leapt away. He looked up to see Whippett staring down at him.

“What the heck happened to you? Get a little jumpy?” Whippett asked laughing, his Adam’s apple sliding up and down in his long neck again.

“Ha, ha!” Calvin laughed sarcastically, “I almost broke my head, and you were going way too fast!”

“Well now, you said you was in a big rush, and heck I was almost halfway there before I seen you was gone. I hate to tell you, but now the price is going to have to be double,” he said firmly.

Calvin felt like popping him one. Instead, he took a long deep breath.

“Look, I’ll pay you double if you drive more carefully and slow down!”

“You got yourself a deal!” said Whippett, smiling proudly, revealing his missing tooth.

Calvin climbed in and checked to see if his bag and backpack were still there. They were, and he pulled out more money. As he handed the bills to Whippett, he told him to wait a minute. Calvin unbuckled his belt; he put one end of it through the slats in the wagon and then brought it back around his waist. He hoped this would hold him inside the wagon this time. He was ready. He felt a little stirring and finally said to Whippett, “Well let’s get going!”

“We are goin’!” answered Whippett.

“What do you mean we’re going? We are barely moving!”

"Well, you told me to slow down!"

"You're tiptoeing, you nut. Move it!" Calvin yelled.

With that, Whippett took off like lightning again. Calvin was bumping up and down, sliding back and forth. Sometimes he was hanging halfway out of the wagon. He held on, praying the belt would not give way. Calvin hurled in midair, but he did not fall out again.

It was the next day when they had finally arrived. He climbed out of the wagon and grabbed his bags, feeling like he had been beaten to a pulp again.

"Thanks a lot," Calvin said sarcastically.

"Hey, buddy," he chuckled bumping Calvin's shoulder with his own, "they don't call me Whippett for nothin'!" Then he zoomed off laughing and cackling like a wild man, leaving Calvin for the second time in a puff of dust. He shrugged it off. He didn't care. Whippett had gotten him where he wanted to go, and he was excited. As he walked through the town he noticed a sign posted in the window of a store. It read:

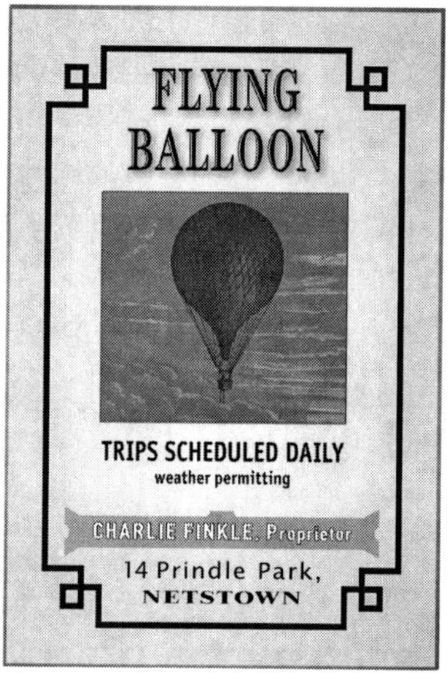

Calvin was in the right place. He rushed inside the store and asked the clerk for directions. The clerk was happy to write them down for him.

"Great!" said Calvin. "I am closer than I thought." He headed off to find Charlie Finkle and his flying balloon. As he approached the hill, he could see the balloon in the distance. "It must be at least twenty feet high," he whispered. It had a small basket at the bottom, which could probably only fit two men. He noticed a man fussing with the balloon. Calvin introduced himself and asked if he was Charlie Finkle.

"Yes, I am, and what can I do for you?" Charlie asked. Calvin explained where he wanted to go and told him he could only find the mountain at dawn when the sun was rising. Charlie told him if they left at midnight and the weather was good and the wind was just right, they should be flying above the mountaintops by sunrise. Calvin was thrilled.

Calvin paid Charlie and they made a plan to meet that night to prepare for takeoff.

After walking through the town most of the day, Calvin found a quiet place under a big tree and decided to take a little nap. Falling off into a deep sleep, he had a dream. In the dream he was standing on a very narrow road. Surrounding him on both sides of the road were huge, dense trees. It began to get very dark. He could not see where he was going, but he felt a gentle wind nudging him along. He looked down and there was a tiny light shining around his feet, giving off enough of a glow to take his next step. As he continued on, he came to a fork in the road. There, before him, were two paths.

One path looked wide and open, the other looked narrow and somewhat hidden. He wanted to go down the wide path. It looked easier, and he thought he saw light beyond, but the gentle wind rose up again, nudging him to go toward the narrow path. Instead, he took a few steps down the wide path, and, at first, it was fine. As he walked further on, he began to feel that it was getting darker. He noticed the light around his feet was gone, and the gentle wind was now passing him by. Suddenly, he felt totally alone. He ran back to where he started and then turned down the narrow path. Still no light shone at his feet, and no gentle wind came to direct him. He began to feel afraid, but continued on down the dark path. When he looked up, even the sky was black.

Now he could not see anything, and he had no idea where he was going. He was becoming more and more fearful. With no one to turn to, he stopped, feeling like his heart was pounding way too fast in his chest. He put his head down, sorry that he went the other way when he knew he was being led to go in the other direction. He looked around again. He did not know where to go, and he needed help.

Suddenly, the black clouds in the sky parted, letting a light shine down on him. The light was so bright, he covered his eyes with his arm, and when he looked up, standing in front of him was what looked to him to be an enormous angel.

Calvin backed away.

"Do not be frightened," the angel said. "Do you understand now?" he asked him.

Calvin answered. "I think I do."

"The wrong way often looks the most inviting. You knew which way you were being led to go, but you went by what you saw." Calvin nodded his head. "God has a great plan for your life, but you have to follow your heart and listen to His guidance. He reveals Himself in many ways. In your heart you will find His answer. But make no mistake Calvin, there are evil forces that want to stop you from finding your true purpose and destiny. Be aware of this, and understand that the choice is always up to you! You will encounter troubles, for He will allow your faith to be tested. However, keep searching, keep believing, and God above will bring you through all your problems, no matter how great they seem to you!" A bright light flashed before him again and the angel was gone.

When Calvin woke up, he remembered his dream vividly. It had seemed so real. He never wanted to forget what the angel had said, so he decided to write it down.

Charlie returned and he began to show Calvin the mechanics of his balloon. The night passed quickly, and soon it was nearing midnight. It was warm with a refreshing breeze in the air.

"Well, I guess we're as ready as we'll ever be," Charlie said.

They each climbed in after Charlie lit the tank that contained the fuel, and as it burned, the balloon began to rise. "Up, up and away,"[8] Charlie exclaimed.

They flew up into the starry-lit night, under the warmth of moon glow. "Wow, what a feeling," Calvin said. He felt as free as a bird.

"Make a wish!" Charlie said, chuckling at Calvin's excitement.

They stared all about them at the gorgeous night. Hours went by as they floated along with the stars. Later, the wind started to grow stronger and the balloon took off swiftly into the depths of the night. Over land and sea, the balloon moved swiftly, as if the wind was guiding them.

Just as Charlie had told him before, as dawn was breaking, they could see the mountains ahead of them. Light began to crack through the clouds, and then he saw it. Directly in back of a distant mountaintop, the beams of sunlight shone and burst out in the shape of a huge star with all the colors of the rainbow. Calvin gasped. "Wow! There is Morningstar Mountain! It's totally incredible!" Calvin said as he looked at it in amazement.

"Now that is really something to see," said Charlie, smiling. "If the weather stays this way, we should be there in a matter of hours."

Calvin was ecstatic. He was almost there. There was just one problem; the weather did not hold out

---

[8] Fifth Dimension. "Up, Up and Away"

that morning. Soon, black clouds rolled in and were all around them. The sky began shooting out huge balls of hail. They were coming down like rocks from the sky. "Say your prayers!" Charlie cried. "If that hail hits the balloon it could burst a hole right through it, and we are going to be knee deep in trouble!"

It wasn't long after he said it, that they heard a loud bursting noise. The hail had hit the balloon and it had blown a big hole in the side of it. They instantly felt themselves starting to drop. Charlie pulled out his knapsack.

"What's that?" Calvin asked with panic in his voice.

Charlie handed him a pocketknife. "Quick, cut the sandbags off," he yelled. Meanwhile, Charlie dressed himself in a vest of some sort and buckled up as Calvin watched in horror.

"What are you doing?" Calvin yelled, feeling the balloon drop a little more.

Charlie began to pull himself up over the basket. "Sorry, kid, I only have one of these safety vests. I couldn't fit another one in the basket!" he said as he hoisted himself up over the edge and jumped, yelling, "Sorry, kid, but you're on your own!"

Calvin was horrified, but there was no time to do anything but start cutting the sandbags as fast as he could. The balloon was whizzing downward now. Soon it would have no air left in it at all and he would just fall. Calvin looked down, which he shouldn't have done. The ground was rushing toward him as the balloon dropped faster and faster. Calvin sat down and held on. He felt himself falling.

"Somebody, help!"

Those were his last words before the balloon started to fall faster and faster, and Calvin just stayed down, grabbing the inside of the basket and holding on for his life. Suddenly, he just crashed. The airless balloon smashed right into the middle of a huge waterfall. He instantly began tumbling and rolling, and the balloon wrapped around the basket, covering him so he could not see a thing. He could feel the water beneath him trying to either push him off or it would crush him to pieces. He felt himself rolling and rolling inside, being knocked around like a twig. Then, suddenly, he was being lifted, and then he was sent crashing under the force of a giant wave, and he could feel himself falling again until he hit the bottom of the crushing waterfall. After that, everything just went black.

Later, and Calvin couldn't tell how long, he woke up. He was still sitting in the balloon basket, but it had been completely covered by the deflated balloon. He could hear birds chirping and water bubbling, but could not see a thing. "Am I dead?" Calvin asked himself out loud. "I don't think so," he answered himself. He realized he was still in the balloon's basket. He tried to push the cover off. He stood up with the balloon still covering him and began pulling and pulling, until he finally came to the end of it and broke free.

He looked around him. He was at the foot of a mountain, next to a waterfall, his bags, still amazingly there. He headed toward the sound of the water. Finally, he came to it. Staring at the huge, rushing waterfall, he could not believe he had survived it. The water, he noticed, seemed to be coming right out of the side of the mountain. He figured it must be Morningstar Mountain, and maybe, if he just kept following around the base of the mountain, he would find the Village.

He began his journey. On the right side of him was a huge, thick forest with dense foliage and enormous trees. On his left loomed the huge mountain. He hadn't walked far before he thought he heard someone calling for help. He stopped to listen. The voice sounded weak but somehow familiar.

"Help, please! Help," the voice cried on.

Suddenly, Calvin recognized the voice. "Charlie," he called back. "Charlie, is that you?" Calvin waited a moment and he heard him again. "Keep talking, Charlie, so I can follow the sound of your voice!"

Charlie moaned and groaned with as much force as he could muster. Calvin ran toward his voice, running deeper and deeper into the forest. But he didn't know that he was not the only one to hear his voice, nor was he the only one trying to find him.[9]

---

[9] Jethro Tull. "Locomotive Breath"

"Hold on, Charlie, I'm coming!" Calvin seemed to be going in circles and still could not find Charlie. "Charlie!" he yelled. "You are going to have to shout as loud as you can for me to find you!" Calvin waited, but heard nothing. He called out his name again and again, and finally he heard it.

"Help! Please, help me!"

In a few moments, he found him. He looked up to see him hanging from the end of a large tree branch, still quite a ways from the ground. The safety vest tangled in the tree. He could see that he was all cut up from the fall, and his clothes were torn.

Calvin pulled out the knife out he had stuck in his belt and quickly began to climb the tree. When he got to the branch, he edged his way out trying to keep his balance as the branch began to bend.

"Hang in there, Charlie, I'm almost there."

Charlie's voice sounded weaker until all he could do was moan. The closer he got to him the more the branch began to dip. "Charlie, if I try to pull you up, the branch will snap! I'm going to have to cut the vest straps, and you are going to fall."

Charlie moaned again. "My leg, I think it's broken."

"I'm sorry, but there is no other choice," he said as he began to saw the straps of the safety vest. "Try to fall on your good side, and the second you're down I'll come to help you, and I'll fix you up good as new. Hold on, now. I'm almost done," he said through gritted teeth. Pulling at the strap with the blade of his knife, he sawed through the final threads.

"It's cut!" he yelled as the strap let loose, and Charlie hit the ground with a howl. Calvin came down from the tree as fast as he could and ran to kneel at his side.

"My leg, my leg!" cried Charlie.

"It'll be all right," said Calvin, trying to calm him down and reassure him. "I'm going to get you some water and then I'll set that leg in a splint, and I'll even make you a cane. Hey, I'll even carry you if I have to," he said as he made a pillow out of his baggage, trying to make him as comfortable as possible. "Charlie, listen to me, you try to rest for a few minutes and I'll be back with some water, and you'll be good as new soon."

Charlie nodded and looked up at him. Sweat poured off of his face, and his eyes were full of pleading.

Calvin made his way back to the brook as fast as he could, looking along the way for the right size piece of wood to make a stint and cane for Charlie. On his way back, he stopped, thinking he had heard a noise. It was a pathetic sound, an evil laughter that did not even sound human. Suddenly a chill ran down his spine. "Oh, God," he thought out loud. "It's not human!"

Then he heard Charlie cry out again, and Calvin ran back to him as fast as he could go. He grabbed a huge branch along the way, not knowing what to expect, just knowing that it was dangerous.

"I'm coming!" he cried as he ran, nearing the place in the forest where he had left Charlie. Then, his worst fears came to life when he saw them. Three brown hyenas, two standing aside, wide-eyed, waiting hungrily for their turn, and one heading right for Charlie's throat.

Calvin's heart was pounding in his chest as he raised the huge branch above his head, and, yelling as loud as he could, he swung the branch in circles, running straight for the hyenas. They each turned to look at him with a fleeting glance of hungry welcome until the animals realized that he was about to attack them.

"Get! Get away from him!!" he shouted, still coming toward them. They would not give in that easily and prepared to attack him until Calvin came upon the hyena that had gotten to Charlie. Drawing the branch down, he swung at the hyena and hit him with such force that he slammed him into the other two.

They gave a loud yelp as they were all knocked off their feet. When the animals gained back their footing, they looked at him, and when they saw him swinging that branch around again, they started to run.

Calvin chased them, still shouting and waving the branch like a madman. The hyenas disappeared into the thickening forest. Calvin stopped and leaned over, trying to catch his breath. He stood a moment, then hurried back to try to help Charlie. He looked down at him lying motionless. He could see the bite marks on Charlie's neck, blood pouring out of the wounds. Calvin tore at his own shirt, and held the cloth over his cuts, trying to stop the bleeding.

"Charlie," he said, speaking softly now. No answer. He tried again and again to rouse him, still nothing. Calvin began to sense that hopeless feeling when someone is slipping away. He felt like sobbing. He put his head down, his hands covering his face.

"Calvin." Charlie's voice was barely audible.

Calvin took his hands away from his face, fearing that he was hearing things as he looked at him. Then hope filled his heart again. "Charlie, you're going to be alright! Please hang in there!" he begged.

Charlie weakly reached for his arm. "Please, listen to me, Calvin."

Calvin knelt down at his side. Charlie coughed and said, "Please, please I'm so sorry, Calvin, for what I did to you," he paused trying to gather strength.

Calvin began to argue, but Charlie held up his hand to stop him.

Isn't life strange," Charlie said with a little chuckle. "It should have been you that was hurt or perhaps dead, because I left you all alone in a very hopeless situation, thinking only of how to save myself. I am so ashamed, Calvin. You risked your life to try to save me, even after what I had done to you," he told him and his voice began to fade. He swallowed hard and went on, "You, friend, are a very courageous man, and I got exactly what I deserve."

Calvin stared shaking his head. "Please, Charlie, you sound like you're giving up. Don't give up," he pleaded.

His face was draining of color as he went on. "I have nothing to show for my life, Calvin. Don't make the same mistakes I did. Make your life matter. Why, there is no one who will even miss me when I'm gone," he whispered. "All I ask is that you forgive me. Is that possible, can you forgive me?"

"Forgive you? Of course I forgive you. Please don't talk like that, Charlie. You have enough to worry about." Calvin stopped and stared at him when he thought he saw a small smile on Charlie's face. Charlie nodded his head slowly.

"Thank you," he whispered, and he died.

Calvin sat a long time in a state of shock. Then he spent the next several hours digging a grave for Charlie, trying his best to give the man a proper burial. Exhausted, he stared down at the little stone mound that contained yet another person that he had to watch suffer and die. He couldn't help but flash back again to his mother and his father.

He looked up toward Heaven. The sky was beginning to darken. Filled with anger that suddenly broke loose, he picked up a rock and smashed it into the mound. "Why does everything I do have to end this way? Everything seems to turn out bad or end in death! Tell me, will there ever be any end to it? Will there ever be any happiness?"

He shook his head, picked up his bags and began to walk toward the stream. He was really tired, sad, weary, and hungry, and dusk was turning quickly to night in an endless, threatening forest. As he walked on, he began to wonder why he was not at the brook yet, or even hearing it. He had been so lost in his own thoughts, he really wasn't paying attention. He began to feel a little nervous, wondering where he was, when suddenly he came upon Charlie's grave. He was right back where he started. Again, he set off and tried to follow the path as carefully as he could remember. He had gotten there so easily before. But, to his bewilderment, he ended up right back at the same place.

It was dark out, and there was barely any moonlight. He was very thirsty. He knew he needed to light a fire. It took him quite a while to find a torch to light so that he could see when he walked. He heard, in the distance, all sorts of wild animal noises. He set off again, this time running, trying all the while to keep the torch lit. He tried as hard as he could to recall which way to go, but, again, he was back at the same place. He was truly frightened now, fearing he would never find his way out, or that perhaps one of the wild animals would find him and he would end up being eaten. His heart pounded harder the more he thought of it. He ran again, trying desperately to find his way out of the woods, only to find he had traveled, again, in a complete circle. Over and over he tried, circling round and round, trying to keep the torch lit, trying to remember the way out of the huge woods, but everything looked the same. His throat had become so dry he could barely swallow. He felt he could not go on much more. His mind was reeling, wondering where he was and why he could not find his way, no matter how hard he tried. He remembered his anger. He stopped and thought how he was really angry at God. He should have thanked him for saving him from the falling balloon, thanked him for saving him from the wild animals. He should have thanked him for a lot of things. He knew, now, why he was going in circles, and he knew it was his turn to ask for forgiveness.

Finally, exhausted, starving, and dying of thirst, he fell to his knees and asked.[10]

[10] Chapman, Gary. "Man after your own Heart"

6
The Village

Calvin woke to the sun shining and the birds singing. He quickly found his way to the streaming, clear brook, and after drinking the cool water, he set out to find the Village. He was so excited to finally be so near Morningstar. He looked around, seeing nothing but forest and trees. He followed the stream toward the falls as he neared, again, the base of the mountain. He walked on for hours, and just as he was beginning to think he had gone the wrong way again, he came upon a huge wall, and then as he traveled on, he came to a gate. He knew he must look like a sight, but he didn't care. As he followed the high iron gate around the bend, he began to be filled with the old excitement and anticipation, hoping that this was really the Village of Morningstar Mountain. After all these years, his lifelong dream might be coming true.

As he came around the corner, he spotted two funny looking men at the entrance of the gate. Uniformed in blue and white, they stood staring straight ahead. Tall blue hats loomed high atop their heads, and they each held a spear, which they clicked together, then crossed to cover the gate as Calvin approached them.

"Excuse me," said Calvin warily, "but am I in the right place? I mean," he swallowed hard, trying to brace himself for the answer, "is this Morningstar Village?"

The guards withdrew their spears and stepped forward. One of the guards stretched his neck toward Calvin and squinted his eyes. "What's it to you?" he asked suspiciously.

Calvin gulped again. "Well, I've traveled a long way to get here and—"

The guard interrupted him immediately as he boldly enunciated each word, holding up his hand to signal a stop sign. "Don't-even-think-about-it! No thugs, no liars or thieves are allowed into the Village. If you're born here, well there is nothing we can do about that, but strays that just come along can just keep right on going! Not even a chance that you are getting into this Village," he exclaimed.

Calvin stood there not sure if he was hearing right at first, and then he started to feel a bit insulted. "Listen, I am not a thug, a liar, or a thief."

"Oh yeah," the guard sneered. "Then prove it!"

"Prove it? How?" Calvin repeated in surprise.

"And that is precisely my point! You can't prove it, and we aren't taking any chances," snapped the guard.

"You don't seem to understand. I am not some stray just casually passing by, I have traveled hundreds of miles, maybe even thousands of miles, I don't know anymore, just to get here, and you're saying I can't enter because I might be a thug?"

"Or a liar, or a thief," the guard shot back.

“Oh, great,” said Calvin angrily, shaking his head. “Ya know, I don’t even,” he paused. He was speechless. “Just forget it.”

“Yes, that sounds fine to me,” the guard said, smirking while the other guard was still staring forward, expressionless.

Calvin just stood there staring for a few moments in shock. He began to shake his head again, not even knowing where he would go. He had never even imagined this ever happening. He couldn’t believe it. Frustration began to rise up inside of him. He thought of Mrs. Tag. He wondered why she hadn’t warned him.

“I should have told Mrs. Tag it all sounded too easy,” he said out loud to himself as he turned to walk away.

“Wait,” the guard said, his ears perking up. “Did you say Mrs. Tag?”

“Yeah,” Calvin answered, not bothering to look back.

The snappy guard glanced over to the other guard. “Hold on a minute,” the guard called after him.

Calvin stopped and turned back to face them.

“You know, I never forget a name. Quick, Henrald, check the big book and see if Mrs. Tag’s name is recorded in it.”

The other guard fetched the big, old, dusty book. He looked through it for what seemed to be forever. Calvin wondered what difference this would make.

“T, T, Tag, yes, yes, here she is. She is written in the book, but she left the Village many, many years ago,” announced Henrald.

"Yes," Calvin said. "Her husband died, and she had to return to her family to raise her son." Calvin reached into his bag and pulled out the amazing rock Mrs. Tag had given him. "She gave me this," he said, holding the jeweled stone out for the guards to see.

The guard's eyes widened. "Yes," he began nodding his head. "Yes, those jewels in that rock can only be found in one place in the world, and that is here! He began to count the layers of the stone revealing each gem out loud." Emerald, peridot, sard, moonstone, lapis, turquoise, amethyst, agate, hyacinth, jasper, carnelian, and chrysotile. They are all here." He announced, looking straight at Calvin.

"But it is really a sad shame about what happened to Mrs. Tag. I remember now, her husband was killed when he left the Village to go into the forest. The wild animals got him when he went searching for the diamond mines. Still, to this day, no one has ever found the diamonds, though many have tried. Poor Mrs. Tag, she was so devastated about losing her young husband, she had to leave the Village. It was just a terrible tragedy, terrible. All of us who live in the Village felt so sorry for her."

The guard sighed deeply, but then he took a deep breath and looked up again at Calvin with a slight grin. "Though it happened very long ago, I am glad you've brought good news that Mrs. Tag is safe. We all wondered what had happened to her. Well , you've convinced me. If Mrs. Tag thought enough of you to send you here and give you that precious rock, then I have complete confidence that you, sir, are a worthy enough man to become a new citizen of Morningstar Village!" The guard placed the book in front of him. "Please sign your name right here," he said, pointing his finger.

Calvin smiled with relief. He took the pen and signed his name in the book.

"You, sir, are now an official citizen of Morningstar Village! Congratulations!"

Henrald stepped forward and said, "In or out, roundabout, give a shout, you got clout! It's no doubt, you're in, not out!"

"Thank you, Henrald, for your welcome speech," said the other guard.

"Welcome speech, life's a beach. I just talk, I don't teach. Grab a star, it's in your reach!"

The other guard rolled his eyes impatiently and said, "Okay, Henrald, enough already. Let's get on with it."

Both guards shook his hand and then, at the same time, they tapped three times on the gate with their spears. The gate opened, and there, sitting at a crystal clear desk, was an older man with dazzling eyes, white hair, and a white beard. He stood up as the guards handed him the official book with Calvin's name written in it. The man at the desk put his seal on it. He then raised both arms, and two men appeared with long trumpet horns. They raised their horns as the bearded man announced, "The people welcome you, Mr. Calvin

Bella, to Morningstar Village, and it is a secret to only the people of Morningstar that this is the edge of the Garden of Eden." As soon as he spoke it, the trumpets sounded and Calvin walked through the gates.

No description, no words could ever have prepared Calvin for the sight he beheld. No, it was more than that; this was where he belonged and he knew it instantly. After years of feeling so alone, he had finally made it, and immediately it felt like he had found a home at last.

The street that wound before him was sparkling and colorful. It was magnificent just like the jeweled rock Mrs. Tag had given him. He had never even imagined that roads could look like this. Overhead, the trees arched all along the way, as if he were walking under a bridge. The cool breeze he felt shook the colorful leaves off the trees almost as if they were applauding for him

Calvin questioned himself, thinking he must be dreaming, but he knew it was finally real. Everywhere were fruit trees. Apples of every variety covered the branches, ripe and ready to be savored. Peaches, apples, oranges, pears, and plums grew in the fields as far as the eye could see on both sides of the fruit laden street. Vines were heavy with assorted big grapes. Bushes were filled with bright berries, and the scent of it all filled the air, leaving a heavenly aroma that swept through the breeze.

It was overwhelming, and Calvin instantly felt renewed as if he was starting life over and this was the first day he felt truly alive.

As he turned the corner, anxious now to see everything, he spotted the festive little Village ahead of him. The quaint Village sat in a semicircular shape with the jeweled streets winding its way in and around the little shops. Directly behind the Village loomed the enormous mountain where Calvin had first been mesmerized by the breathtaking sunrise and the morning star.

Calvin jumped up and snatched a bright red, perfect apple. Then he picked a few plump, ripe berries and popped them in his mouth. The apple was so crisp, and the berries were sweet and juicy. He could feel the fruit instantly energize his body. He didn't know where to look first, trying to take in all the beauty. He took a few steps forward, and then he'd circle back around, not wanting to miss a thing, enchanted by everything that surrounded him. Even the air seemed somehow different; lighter, fresher, and lovely.

When he arrived in the Village, he saw, in the very center, a pond surrounded by grass that was so green it looked blue.

A tall man with a very wide mustache was playing a mandolin there. A woman stood by his side jingling a tambourine. Another man played the violin, and one had a harmonica. Another man sat at the drums. They were watching him, and Calvin smiled.

"Hi, I'm Calvin Bella," he said, holding out his hand.

"Call me Uncle Peter, everyone does," he said with a laugh in his voice, "and this is my wife, Leelee." He returned Calvin's handshake and gestured to the guys in the band. Immediately, they began to play.

"Calvin Bella, how do you do? Calvin Bella, we welcome you. It's nice to see such a fine young man stroll into town to shake our hand." They all laughed. Uncle Peter took a bow, and Leelee curtsied, and they told Calvin to come by any time.

Calvin looked around the little town. There were all sorts of little shops, each one connected to the next. All of them were quaint, yet colorful and unique. They each had their own sign and Calvin read them; Bubbles Ice Cream Palace, Bully's Brides and Gowns, Itchy's Laundry, Big Daddy's Lollipop Shop, Karess's Bed and Breakfast Inn, Classy's Café, Dredge's Newsstand, Bones Malt shop, Tete's Tango Hut, Bubu's Beauty Shop, Carlton's Fine Dining at Nine, Flip's Floats, and, finally, Hedda's Bakery. *Hmmm, funny names,* he thought. He could smell something delicious cooking and he thought it was coming from the bakery, so he decided to go in there first.

"Hey, man, what's happening? I'm Hedda," the man said when he walked in, and held out a hand toward Calvin. "Hey, could you smell my cookin' out there," the man asked eagerly. He had a tight-fitting thin, black sock over the top of his head and wore dark, small, round glasses that he looked over when he spoke.

"Oh, yeah, it smells great," answered Calvin as he introduced himself and returned the handshake. Calvin couldn't help but turn his gaze to all the cookies, cakes, pies, breads, and creamy little puffs.

"Well, you are just in time, I am just about to take my newest recipe out of the oven," he said as he reached in to pull out his masterpiece. "I call this 'the cream of the crop.' Grew every ingredient right outside my back door. Everything is fresh, fresh, fresh; couldn't be any fresher! Come," Hedda said, motioning to Calvin to take a seat. "Come and taste."

Calvin was more than happy to take a bite. "Mmm, delicious."

"You like?" Hedda said, delighted and nodding. "Here, try this cream-stuffed puff. It's on the house. I need an objective opinion."

Calvin sunk his teeth into the chocolate-covered cream stuff. "Wow! It's fantastic," was all he could manage while his mouth was filled with pastry, whipped cream, and chocolate.

"Unreal, isn't it," Hedda said proudly.

"Unreal," Calvin agreed as he savored the last bite.

"So, you got a place to crash with us here in the Village?"

"Crash?" asked Calvin, confused.

"You know, a place to stay?"

"Oh," Calvin laughed. "Ah, no, not yet. Got any suggestions?"

"Well, Karess's Bed and Breakfast Inn is nice, and so is Karess," he smirked.

"I guess I should go over and see if she's got a room to rent then," said Calvin.

"Hey," Hedda said, holding his hand out to Calvin again, "It was great to meet you, Cal. Come by anytime and we'll do lunch."

Calvin returned the handshake. "I will definitely do that, thank you, Hedda," he said as he walked toward the door.

"Anytime, Cal," he said, waving. "By the way, I'm cooking dream cups tomorrow. They are one of my favorites. Should you forget, don't worry; you'll smell them cooking."

Calvin smiled back at Hedda. "Hey, believe me, I won't forget your cookin'. See ya tomorrow."

Calvin walked down the street toward Karess's Bed and Breakfast. People were scurrying all about. He noticed something funny coming toward him: three girls who seemed to have the same face, walking side by side, but he couldn't make out what was above their heads. It looked like they had a big black cloud hovering over them.

Calvin strained to get a better look. He realized they were triplets, and it wasn't a black cloud over their heads, it was their hair! He had never seen anyone with so much hair. It was so high and wide, he wondered if it felt heavy on their heads. As they approached, he stepped aside to let them and their hair pass by. He smiled politely and they giggled at him. As they walked on, he noticed that tagging right behind them was a fat, black and white cat and a tiny, brown poodle. The cat meowed at Calvin, and the dog barked.

"Stop that, Footie and Skunky!" said one of the triplets to the cat and the dog. She turned to Calvin. "Just ignore Footie and Skunky, they aren't use to strangers," she said.

"Oh, not a problem," said Calvin.

"Who are you, if you don't mind us asking?"

I'm new here. The name is Calvin, Calvin Bella, and I just arrived here today."

"Are you here to stay?" asked one triplet. "Do you like it here?" asked the other triplet. "You're just visiting aren't you?" asked another.

"Ummm, yes, yes, and no," he pointed at each one as he answered, and they all burst into laughter.

"Actually, I'm hoping to make this my home," said Calvin happily.

They all huddled and whispered and giggled before one said, "Well then, let me introduce you. This is Swobinia, and that is Birdinia, and I am Beakinia, but everyone calls us Swobbie, Birdy, and Beaky. And, of course, you met our dog, Foot, and our cat, Skunk, nicknamed Footie and Skunky.

Calvin studied them, and wondered how he would ever be able to tell who was who. "Let me see, now," he said, "it's Swobbie, Beaky, Birdy, Skunk, and Footie, right?"

"You got it!"

Suddenly, Swobbie took out a mirror and began smiling in it while holding it at arm's length. It looked as if she were posing. He could not help looking when he saw her checking her lip color while smacking her lips together several times, and then puffing up her hair, not noticing that anyone else was around. She seemed totally enraptured by watching herself in the mirror. He stared at her, and tried to act like this was all normal.

"Well, it's nice to have met you," he said as he looked at Swobbie while she tried out different expressions in the mirror. He caught himself staring again, and turned his attention to their dog and cat.

"Ah, say, is there any special reason why you named your dog Footie, and your cat Skunk? I mean, ah, they're great names they're just, ah, very unique."

"Well," Beaky began, "Footie just can't seem to stop biting everyone's toes, you see. I keep telling Birdy," with her voice getting louder, "'KEEP YOUR SHOES ON!' But she doesn't listen, so we are always mending up her toes. We don't know why, but that's Footie for ya, and she's always been like that, so you can guess why we just had to name her Footie."

"Oh, yeah," Calvin nodded in agreement. "I see your point."

"Now, Skunk, on the other hand, well, we call her Skunk because she thinks she is one. It's all we can do to keep her away from skunks in the woods." She whispered now, "She's gotten sprayed at least six times, and the smell, you just can't imagine! But it doesn't faze her a bit; I think she's actually happy about it. Anyway, we don't mention the word C-A-T around her unless we whisper. You get what I mean?"

"Oh, yeah, definitely, I get what you mean," said Calvin, trying to hide his amazement.

Calvin looked over at Swobbie, who was still looking in the mirror, while Beaky went on about bandaging toes and skunk smell remover. Swobbie began raising her eyebrows up and down, smiling and checking all her teeth, then pursing her lips and turning her head from side to side as if she wanted a look from all angles. Suddenly, she brought her head down to her knees, and then flipped her hair back, and then Beaky and Birdy did the same! Calvin stepped back, their hair even higher now. He felt tempted to say, "Wow, you girls got some big hair," but he thought it would be rude, and the girls were actually very nice. Swobbie looked back in the mirror to check her big hair.

"So do you need a job?" asked Birdy.

"Yes, I do," Calvin answered. "I was planning on looking for one tomorrow."

"Well, our Daddy is rich and he owns the wheel factory and all the land in Morningstar," they boasted. "We'll be glad to put in a good word for you. He's always looking for a good worker and all that voity toity," said Birdy.

"That would really be nice of you. I'll go over first thing in the morning." They gave him directions and he promised to be there. "Thank you, Birdy, Beaky and Swobbie." He felt strange saying their unique names.

Swobbie came out of her trance with the mirror when she heard him say her name. "Oh, huh?" What?" she asked.

"Thank you, it was nice to meet you," Calvin repeated.

"Oh, of course, nice to meet you too," Swobbie replied nodding her head. The friendly girls with the cloud began to drift away, and he thought he heard them arguing.

"He was looking at me the most!"

"No, he was looking at me the entire time!"

"Don't you think this lip color looks the best on me?"

"Oh voity, toity!"

Calvin couldn't help laughing as he walked on toward Karess's Inn. When he walked in, a tall blonde with a long, tight, red dress, red fingernails, and ruby red lips immediately greeted him.

Calvin asked her if he could speak with Karess.

"You're lookin' at 'er, pumpkin. And what can I do for you?" she asked enthusiastically. Calvin explained that he needed a place to stay, and she told him she was more than happy to rent him a room. She immediately offered him the featherbed suite. He told her not to go to any trouble that any room would do for now. "How long do you plan on staying in the Village?" Karess asked with a long southern style drawl.

"Forever, I hope, if not longer!" he said.

"Well, that's just great! Why that's gotta be the greatest news I've heard in a few decades! Don't you worry your li'l ol' self, sweetie. I'm charging you the same price as I charge for the smaller rooms. It's just so nice to have a young, strong, handsome man around here, *tsk, tsk*."

She led him up to the room.

"Now we're going to make you real, real... comfortable," she told him slowly, lowering her voice. *Tsk, tsk*.

The next morning, after Karess cornered him for a half an hour, he was finally able to get out the door without seeming impolite. He set out to try to get the job at the wheel factory. He managed to get right in to see the man known as Mr. Biffer Snip, and he knew he could thank the triplets for that.

He was a big man; bald, with spectacle glasses. He talked very fast and got right to the point. After speaking with him for no more than ten minutes, Calvin had gotten himself a job and would start the first of next week at six o'clock sharp.

Feeling elated, he walked back to the Village Center. There, he saw two geese and three ducklings crossing the jeweled street. He stopped to watch them, and he saw them jump right into the little pond.

He headed down the fruit-laden street again and ate some blueberries and then decided on a peach and a pear. Each fruit tasted better than the last. He walked along the outskirts of the Village, trying to see it all. Surrounding the Village was rolling green grass. All about him were flowering trees and bushes of every type and color; deep lavenders and reds, purples, pinks and the whitest of whites, yellows, oranges, and light shades of pastels.

Blue jays, cardinals, parrots, canaries, and fluffy white birds all habitated within the lush foliage. The birds were all singing their own song as the butterflies gracefully danced.

Calvin was in awe. He was amazed at the harmony there. He just sat down and stared at all the beauty around him. In the distance, he could hear the sound of water. He began to walk toward it. As he drew closer, he thought he could hear laughter. He came upon a stream that led to a small waterfall. The water was turquoise and surrounded by huge, red hibiscus flowers.

There were four girls swimming in the stream, each taking turns climbing up the rocks on the side of the falls, and sliding back down in the waterfall. He watched them laughing and splashing and he thought he heard something very familiar. It was the sound of someone's laughter, and it was enchanting him. He knew he had heard it before, but he didn't know where. He strained to look at the dark-haired beauty with the laugh like a song. He didn't want to startle them; they were having such fun.

Calvin jumped a little when one of them came up behind him and said hi.

"Oh, hi, I'm sorry, I didn't mean to interrupt. I'm new here and I was just exploring," he said.

"The more the merrier, you're welcome to swim too," she said. "I'm Stacey, Stacey Boom, and over there is Kell Starr and Suey Sassay."

They both looked up to see the girl slide down the falls. "And the one coming down the waterfall is Crystalina."

"Crystalina," Calvin repeated in a whisper.

"Yeah," Stacey nodded. "Crystalina Devine."

Calvin felt warmth wash over him and a chill run down his spine even at the sound of her name. And suddenly he felt a stirring inside his heart, like a voice within, but it was clear, and he heard it; a still, small voice speaking to his heart, answering the question he had yet to even ask.

Yes, Calvin, she's the one.

7
Nightmares

It was always the same. First it started with a feeling of pressure, like fingers squeezing her throat. She would try to cry out, but no sound would come. She couldn't breathe. She thought she was dying as she listened to her mind screaming, *Help!* Then a voice beyond the screams… It was her father and she could hear him calling for her with a sound of desperation in his voice.

She realized then, when she opened her eyes, that no one was squeezing her throat, but rather she was suffocating in heavy black smoke that was filling her bedroom. Wrenching coughs were pushing their way out as she tried to sit up on her bed, but every time she inhaled she'd breathe in more smoke. She watched the flames beginning to engulf the walls of her room, and she knew she had only minutes. Then she heard her father's calls again, sounding more desperately frantic than before.

"Crystalina! I'm coming for you!"

She couldn't answer.

Suddenly, her father appeared through the smoke and carried her out to safety, only to turn around and head back into the house that was now engulfed in flames.

She watched in horror and shock and then began to scream, "Daddy!" She watched helplessly as the burning building rose up in a whirlwind of flames and she saw the roof collapse and cave in on her father.

Then she'd wake up, covered in sweat and fear, her heart pounding. It took her a long time to calm herself down. She used to run into her parents room and stay with them for the night, but as the years went by she learned that she would have to calm herself down by telling herself that it was only a nightmare. But it wasn't.

It had been ten years since that horrible night. But night after night, her nightmares would make her relive the horror of it like it were happening all over again. She wanted to forget it—wipe it out of her memory and pretend it never even happened at all. She finally had to accept the fact that her mind would not let her ever forget, and even now she recalled every detail.

They had all been sleeping, and somehow their beautiful home had caught on fire. Her father had rescued her and brought her out safely and into her mother's waiting arms. Then, they both watched as her father ran back into the burning house to get a few precious belongings and the moneybag he had saved. Kissy, their brave little dog went in right after him, and Crystalina tried to run to catch him, but her mother held her back with all her might. Helplessly, they stood watching, waiting; every second lasted and lasted. It was too much to bear. Then, only minutes later, they saw the back of the roof collapse, and then whole house began to cave in on him and their tiny little white puppy dog that she loved so much.

She didn't know, even to this day, if it had been her screaming that roused the neighbors, or if they could smell the smoke in their sleep, but suddenly, men were running toward them, carrying buckets of water, and she watched as they bravely ran right into the burning house to save her father.

Crystalina pulled away hard to go with them, but she could not escape her mother's grasp. It seemed like an eternity as they stood there, watching the flames overtake the whole place, and listening to the crackle of the hungry fire as it snapped, sending sparks flying in all directions. Any second now, she secretly thought, one of them would run out and tell them the worst possible news, and Crystalina knew that she could not take it, that she could not endure hearing the words she feared most in the entire world.

She knew deep inside, beyond any doubt, that she had the best parents in the world. Her father was a star to her, as comforting as a big teddy bear and as kind and generous as Santa Claus. There was no one like him, and she knew this, in the entire world, and it seemed to her that everyone that met him felt the same way.

She was their only child. One of her favorite memories had been when father had brought her home a surprise for her birthday. It was a covered picnic basket decorated in bows, and when he handed it to her she could feel the basket wiggling. She quickly opened the top of it and saw a tiny, white, fluffy head shyly peeking up at her. Instantly she fell in love with the little white dog. She picked her up, and everyone gathered round her saying how cute and little the puppy was as they all tried to pat her. She put her over her shoulder, and the dog laid its head upon it.

"She must not even weigh a pound," Crystalina announced. "I've never seen such a cute little doggy in my life!"

It was then that the little dog lifted its head and began to give tiny, little licks to the side of her cheek. "We'll call her Kissy," she said, laughing as the dog tickled her face. "Oh, Daddy! You have no idea how much this little dog means to me. Thank you, thank you," she said as she went over to hug him.

People were always stopping by the house just to say hello and hang around. Her father took the utmost pleasure in the smallest things. He would sit in his favorite chair, trying out a new flavor lollipop, his false teeth sitting on a table beside him and his sunglasses on. He would tell people that wearing his sunglasses made him feel like he was a star, and then he'd follow that with a jolly laugh. It would make everyone else laugh too, especially since he said it without his teeth in his mouth.

All these memories came back to her instantly as they frantically waited and waited to see if her father and her little dog could be saved. “Please, God,” she prayed out loud, “save them!”

As the wooden house was being consumed, she knew it would take a miracle. Only a flicker of hope remained in her heart, and the more she stared at the huge blaze before her, she knew there wasn’t much of a chance. She buried her head into her mother and began to sob uncontrollably, when, suddenly, she heard her mother saying something. She looked up at her.

“Look!” her mother cried as she pointed her finger toward the house.

She turned to see as the men fought their way out. Two of them were carrying her father. She held her breath. She just stood there, frozen in fear, as they dragged him onto the front grass. They began trying to give him air, and she could see the men were doing all they could. She watched as one man bent down and put his ear to her father’s chest. Then he moved up to his face.

She heard her mother’s sobs when she cried, “oh no, oh no, no, no...”

Crystalina noticed that one of his legs looked bent in a grotesque way. She thought she would be sick. Then she saw one of the men yelling something. She strained her ears to hear him over the blaze, then she heard the magical words, “He’s alive!”

Before they even got to say anything to him, the men interrupted as they spoke about his misshapen leg. They quickly picked him up again and whisked him off as quickly as they could go. A few moments later, she heard the familiar sound of Kissy coming around from the back of the house. She ran to pick her up and cuddled her close. “Oh, thank God, Kissy. You’re okay, and Daddy is alive! Thanks to the Good Lord!” Kissy barked, agreeing with her completely.

The whole house and just about everything in it were burnt up. Crystalina and her mother were sad, but they were so grateful that her father was alive and so was Kissy. That’s all that seemed to be important. No place would be a home without them, and any place could be home as long as they had each other.

Crystalina and her mother had moved to her Aunt Leelee and Uncle Peter’s house, which had been down the street from their own. Her father had to stay in bed for almost three months. Crystalina remembered her shock the first time she saw her father’s leg; it had been amputated at the knee. The doctor told them that, during the fire, a beam smashed down right on his leg, crushing it, and if he didn’t cut it off, her father would die from infection. It was definitely a time of loss; their lovely home, all their belongings, and, worst of all, her father’s leg.

With no money left at all, her parents were forced to sell the land that their house had been built upon to Biffer Snip. Crystalina could not figure out why he needed more land. After all, he owned almost every piece of land in Morningstar. As a matter of fact, when she thought about it, he owned just about everything in

Morningstar. He practically ran the whole Village. Any land that he was ever willing to sell was priced so high that no one she knew could ever afford to buy it.

Biffer Snip built a lot of small homes that were connected to one another, and almost all the people were forced to pay rent in one of Snip's homes. Many of the people called him the town tyrant. If he liked you, he would give you a reasonable rent to pay, but if he didn't, he would keep raising your rent until you were forced to leave Morningstar altogether. Fortunately for Crystalina and her family, Biffer Snip liked them a lot. At least for the time being.

Crystalina rose from her bed and tried to push the nightmare out of her mind. She still hoped one day they would stop.

She was leaning over the top of her bureau to get a closer look in the mirror when she heard someone coming up the stairs. She peered through the mirror to see who was walking through the doorway. It was her best friend, Stacey.

"What are you doing?" asked Stacey as she came into the bedroom.

Crystalina smiled back at Stacey through the mirror's reflection. "I'm trying to see what's wrong with me. You know, I've been thinking. All the girls have a boyfriend except me," she said, turning toward her.

Stacey laughed, "You could have any boyfriend you want. You're just not interested in them."

"Like who, Dapper Snip?" she asked. "He's too spoiled, always running to his rich daddy for everything. I want someone strong who can make it on their own. I guess you could say that I want a *real man*."

Stacey couldn't help laughing again. "Look at you, with your endlessly long dark curls and those green eyes! Why, you are beautiful, Crystalina! You just haven't met the right one for you yet, but he'll find you. You'll see. It'll happen." Stacey told her, trying to reassure her friend. "As a matter of fact, that new guy, Calvin, seemed to have noticed you."

Crystalina looked directly into Stacey's eyes, then caught herself and looked away quickly. She didn't want to admit that she had been thinking of him a lot, ever since she saw him at the waterfall. She felt sort of embarrassed to admit she'd been thinking of someone she hadn't even actually met yet. So, she decided not to say anything.

Crystalina and Stacey had been best friends all their lives. They both grew up in Morningstar and had no idea the rest of the world wasn't nearly as beautiful, bountiful and lush as Morningstar Village, many people tried to tell them, but they simply could not comprehend how blessed they were to grow up in their little enchanting Village.

Stacey walked over to look at the pretty fabric gathered around Crystalina's sewing machine. "Are you making this for the dance?" asked Stacey.

Crystalina's eyes beamed as she walked over and took the material to lay it all out for Stacey. "Yes," she answered. "What do you think?"

"I think it will be simply magnificent! I don't know where you learned to sew like that," Stacey said as she ran her hand across the silk and velvet material.

They were both really excited about the upcoming dance. It was one of the biggest events ever held in the little Village.

Suddenly, they could hear laughter coming from downstairs. It was her mother and her aunt, Jayja.

Crystalina said, "You know, Mama taught me all about cleaning, sewing, washing. You know, she is still comparing her wash with the neighbors, she tells me that, 'They don't know how to wash clothes,' and then she'll say, 'Look, Crystalina. Look at this washing. Why, mine is as white as milk!'" They both burst out laughing when they thought about her mother, Rose.

Rose did not grow up in Morningstar. She grew up in a poor family, in a gray town where people struggled just to put food on the table. Crystalina would sigh to herself when she remembered her mother telling her she never even had a doll to play with. Many times Rose relived the story of her sad childhood to her daughter, repeating how she had to stay home and sew baseballs to help the family earn a living. Crystalina felt sorry for her when she talked of how terribly strict her father had been. It wasn't until Harry Devine came to the town on business that life turned around for the petite, little, red-headed Rose.

The minute he saw her, he knew she was the one for him. Rose liked him instantly too. What started out as a business trip for Harry, ended up to be a time of whirlwind romance for him and Rose. Eventually, he convinced her to come with him back to Morningstar, and it was in the Village that they decided to marry. Rose's sister, Leelee, came to Morningstar to be at her sister's wedding. Leelee met Peter at the wedding, and she was married too.

Harry bought Rose everything she wanted, but never dreamed she'd ever have, a home, lovely furniture, beautiful clothes and supported them well when he opened up his candy business called, 'Big Daddy's lollipop shop.'

Rose was fascinated with all of it, and was determined to keep everything *just so*, she would say, but what that really meant was *immaculate*. She did everything with a passion. If she was cold, she clapped her hands together and exclaimed, "Oh, Harry, I-AM-ICED!" Or if she thought someone lost weight, she would cry out, "Harry! Look!" So and so "got thin as a rail!" Of course, Harry would agree completely.

She was always keeping herself busy. She would dust and clean and organize and wash and rinse, and everything would gleam. She would wear herself out, and even when she'd get tired and cranky, Harry would exclaim, "There goes my flower, Rose!"

Shortly after Rose gave birth to Crystalina, she wrote a letter to her sister, Jayja, inviting her to come to Morningstar. Jayja was on the next train. The minute she arrived, she fell in love with the Village and decided she could never go back to the old, gray place she had grown up in. Jayja stayed with Rose and Harry, and one day they got the news that Mr. Snip's wife had died giving birth to triplets, and he also had a three year old son named Dapper. They felt very sad for him, but that gave Jayja an idea. A few months after the triplets were born, she went to see Mr. Biffer Snip. She asked if he would be interested in a governess to care for his home and children. Biffer looked at her like she was saving his life. He hired her instantly, and Jayja moved to the enormous home of the Snips. He gave her a wing in the house, and soon Jayja began to get everything running smoothly, and she took care of those children as if they were her very own, and Snip was pleased.

Stacey and Crystalina listened to the two women chatting at the kitchen table.

"So, Rosie, how are ya?" Aunt Jayja asked, always sounding as if she were on the verge of a good laugh.

"Half dead!" Rose answered, as she spooned her hot cup of tea.

Crystalina and Stacey giggled when they heard them. It was their usual conversation while having tea at the table; they'd compare stories as to who was doing what work, and they'd console each other along the way.

"Oh, you poor kid, you must be exhausted! You really started your house work at 4 A.M. this morning?" Aunt Jayja asked.

"All I do is go, go, and go!" answered Rose.

"Oh, don't I know it," cried Jayja. "Between the three girls and Dapper, I go crazy! Swobbie doesn't get out of that Mirror! Beaky is downtown spending and spending, and Biff gives those kids anything they ask for. The crazy cat is chasing skunks around the clock, and Footie is always biting Birdie's toes. I'm telling you, Rose, I don't know how I do it! They have me out of my mind!" She told her sister, laughing. "Do you know that with the dance coming up, those three girls have bought five dresses each? And they keep changing their mind. Nothing is ever good enough!" she exclaimed and roared with laughter.

Jayja looked up toward the sky while Rose shook her head.

"You know what I would say to them, don't cha?"

Jayja looked back at her questioningly. "What?"

"Sew a few hundred baseballs!" exclaimed Rose.

And with that, Jayja and Rose started roaring with laughter again. "Could you even picture Swobbie trying to sew a baseball?" They roared with laughter again at the thought of it, "Oh I love those kids. They're like my own. If it wasn't for them—" and she laughed again.

Suddenly, Jayja remembered Harry was in the parlor. "Hey, I almost forgot to say hello to Harry!"

Jayja got up and walked toward the parlor where Harry sat in his usual chair, trying out his new flavor of lollipop, his teeth not in and his sunglasses on. Jayja was fired-up with energy, and yelled to Harry, "How the heck are ya?"

"Excellent!" said Harry. "Just perfect," which was how Harry always was. Rose followed Jayja and sat on the sofa. Just then, the doorbell rang, and it was Aunt Leelee.

Suddenly, Jayja got so happy and excited that she started singing, and soon, the three sisters were up and doing a dance they had learned from their childhood as Harry clapped with the beat.

Crystalina and Stacey ran down to watch the performance. They loved when the Aunts started dancing.

Jayja lifted her long skirts a little to reveal her heavily veined legs, while the other two followed her lead. They sang, "Nynee, nynee, ny-nee-ny, alla-boomp, alla-boomp." Every time they did the "alla-boomp," part, they rolled their hips from side to side. They twirled and swayed and boomped on and on, they curtseyed and bowed and added a few dos-à-dos, until they all fell to the sofa with hilarious laughter. Life was good!

A couple days later, Crystalina decided to bring her dress over to Bully's Bridal shop to see if Bully would help her put the finishing touches on the dress she had made. As she walked along the pretty jeweled streets, she thought of the young man she had seen at the water.

Calvin was his name. She had only seen him from a distance, but she was surprised to find herself thinking of him over and over again.

She looked up and spotted the "Snip trips," as everyone called them, as she entered the dress shop.

"Hi, Crystalina," they said in unison as she walked in.

"Hi, girls!" she said, smiling. "Are you here getting your dresses for the dance?"

"Yeah, but we can't decide which one is the best!" answered Birdy.

"Shhh," Bully exclaimed. "Swobbie is coming out any second to model my very latest creation! Then Swobbie swept back the curtain and came out twirling, flaring the edges of the dress, and stopped in a very poised pose. Bully could hardly contain herself. She beamed as she said, "Absolutely stunning! Yup, that's the dress, girls, without a doubt. And do you know I created this dress out of colored paper and ribbons?"

The girls looked at her in shock. "We are going to wear dresses made of paper?" asked Birdy in horror.

"Yes!" cried Bully ecstatically as she put her hands on her cheeks. "It's all the rage in Europe."

"I knew it!" said Swobbie, looking elated as she stood before them curtsying and bowing, then, back to the mirror, adjusting her dress a bit. She stepped back and forth and side to side, the other two sisters agreeing and clapping, each asking for a dress just like hers.

"Oh, de-finite-ly!" answered Bully, as she tried to put on a European accent. "I'll get busy on them right away." Then she turned back to Swobbie, who was enthralled with her new dress and could not pull herself out of the mirror. Bully was Swobbie's biggest fan, because she did look good with her small waist in everything Bully designed.

"Oh, Swobbie, I can't get over that dress on you!" Bully exclaimed again with her deep voice that seemed to run out of air as she spoke. Crystalina wanted to take a breath for her.

Everyone was so excited, they could hardly wait. Beaky turned back to Crystalina, who had been sitting there watching the whole production with her dress on her lap. "Hey, have you seen that new guy, Calvin, yet? He's going to be working for daddy, ya know… Have you seen him yet?" she asked again. Not giving Crystalina a chance to answer, she added, "Have you? He's gorgeous! Isn't he, girls?" Beaky asked, turning back to her sisters.

"Oh, voity toity! Is that all there is to talk about? I mean, Crystalina, this is all I've heard them talk about for days!" snapped Birdy.

"Voity toity yourself, you know he is!" said Beaky, snapping back at Birdy. She then asked again, but quietly, "Well, have ya seen him?" Beaky raised her eyebrows at Crystalina.

"Well, I guess you could say that. I saw him from a distance at the little waterfall, I mean," she hesitated, not wanting them to know that she had noticed him too. "I guess he was just walking around, and you know, I just, I saw him while we were swimming the other day. You know what I mean. From a distance."

"*Well*, what did you think?" asked Beaky again.

Crystalina did not have time to answer, because Birdy announced suspiciously, while crossing her arms, "He staying at Karess's, ya know."

Suddenly, they all turned to look at Swobbie, who was still modeling for herself in the mirror. She broke out into a song and watched herself perform, her voice rising to the top of her lungs while she sang.

"Sing it, liver! Sing it out strong, liver lips!" Beaky yelled, teasing her sister.

They all broke into hysterical laughter, including Swobbie, although in between laughs she whined, "Hey, my lips don't look like liver! Do they?" she asked as she looked closer to inspect her mouth. Then she started puckering and puffing out her lips over and over while watching herself in the mirror.

This made them all just about fall on the floor in hysterics.

"No, liver! They're perfect liver lips," answered Beaky again as she laughed and laughed and laughed.

Bully was laughing too; one long, continuous laugh that went on and on until she ran out of breath. Crystalina laughed too, but couldn't help but wonder to herself as she watched Bully, *Why doesn't she ever breathe right, or take a breath in between?* It was like watching a balloon with a big leak. Then she had to stop and think, and remind herself of why she went there in the first place.

8
Lollipops and Witches

Everything Calvin had seen in Morningstar had astounded him, and he wanted to see it all. He was simply in awe. Even the people were unique and funny, but the one person he could not stop thinking about was Crystalina. He wanted to meet her, to see her up close. He had to admit to himself he was drawn to her since the moment he had seen her, even from a distance. He remembered hearing that she worked at Big Daddy's Lollipop Shop. He headed that way.

He looked outside the little shop's window before mustering up the courage to go inside. They actually had every kind of candy imaginable, including taffy that was rolled out in thick, long, stretchy pieces. There were gumdrops and sweet tarts, and chocolate molded into shapes, dipped in coconut and nuts. Calvin couldn't help noticing all the different lollipops displayed around the window.

He stepped inside, and he wasn't expecting to see her the moment he opened the door. She was up on a ladder and she turned to face him.

"Hi, um, I'll be right with you," she said, hesitating for a moment to get a long look at this new, mysterious man in town. "I was just putting—"

"Oh, don't hurry on my account," he interrupted her nervously.

Crystalina stepped down from the ladder and walked toward him, smiling. "I'm Crystalina Devine," she offered politely. "I think we saw each other the other day at the waterfall, but I didn't get a chance to introduce myself."

Calvin looked into her green eyes that were framed with long, dark lashes, and suddenly felt like reaching out and touching her long dark hair that fell loosely down her back and curled around her lovely face like a frame. He felt tall next to her, and he loved the sound of her voice that, to him, sounded like a melody.

"I'm Calvin. Calvin Bella," he told her, and caught himself staring at her a little too long. "Well," he said, "I thought I would stop in and meet some of the people."

"Yes, I heard that you were going to be staying here now," she said softly.

"Well, anyone who has seen this place would be crazy not to want to stay. I still can't get over the beauty of it and I haven't even begun to see everything," he said.

"Well, maybe I could show you around," she said, smiling. "I bet I know all the best places in Morningstar."

"I bet you do too," he agreed. "That would be fantastic! When do you think you might have time?"

"Well, tomorrow I am out of work by, say, three."

"Three is perfect. Should I meet you here?" he asked.

"Yes, that sounds great," she answered.

Calvin looked around the little candy store. "You know, I think I'll get something sweet to bring home tonight," he said.

Crystalina laughed. "Oh, a sweet tooth, huh? Well, tell me, what looks good to you?"

"Ah, good question. Everything looks good. What would you choose?"

"Um, I guess it would have to be this," she said, putting a multicolored pretty lollipop on the counter. She laughed at her choice. "This really does taste good, and it lasts a long time."

Calvin nodded his head. "Yes," he said, quietly agreeing. "That's a good choice." He stared at the lollipop that she had put on the counter for a long time. It was the same one his mother had bought for him on the very last day they had been together.

"Calvin," she said gently. "Is everything alright?"

"Yes," he answered, not realizing how long he had been lost in his memories. "I was just remembering something," he hesitated another moment. "Well, I'll take that lollipop, Crystalina," he said. "It was really, really great to meet you, and I'll be here right at three sharp tomorrow."

Calvin walked out the door into the bright sunlight of Morningstar. Taking a deep breath, he said out loud but to himself, "Crystalina, Crystalina… Even her name is beautiful."

Karess was dressed in her usual bright, tight-fitting, long dress, with her sky-high heels. Today they were red, of course, to match her red dress, her lip color, and her long manicured nails. She always hated going to see the witch. But, what other choice did she have? She needed another potion, and she needed it bad. She made her way through the dark, haunting woods, down the small, secret path she had followed so many times before.

"Ouch, ooh, ouch!" she repeated as her shoes sunk in the dirt, twisting and turning her ankles as she walked along.

Her mind was made up. She was taking no chances with this one. He was the most gorgeous hunk of a man she had ever seen, and come hell or high water, she was not letting this one go. She was fixing to make sure that Calvin would be hers and only hers, at any cost. She would see to it.

The day began to darken as she hobbled along while the woods grew thicker. Then she heard a swishing sound over her head. "Oh! My Lord! What the heck was that, a bat?" she asked herself, breathing harder. She hurried along faster now, hoping, through each painful step, that she would spot the witch's house. As she rounded a corner, she suddenly felt the heel of her shoe break right off. "Oh no!" she cried as she took off her flattened shoe. "Damn shoe!" She was startled when someone spoke.

"Hello."

Karess was shocked. "What? Who are you?" She looked ahead of her, and there sat a man on a donkey, right in the middle of the forest, who had seemed to appear out of nowhere.

"Where are you going?" asked the stranger.

Karess was taken aback, and suddenly began to get very nervous. She just stared at him with wide eyes, not answering his question.

"I came to warn you," he announced gently.

"Warn me?" she asked, getting more and more alarmed and confused as she stood there, wide-eyed, holding her broken shoe in her hand.

"Yes, to warn you," he repeated. "You're on your way to visit the witch again, aren't you?" He didn't wait for a response from her. "I came to tell you that witches and witchcraft of any kind—black or white, or any form of craft—comes from a power of darkness, one that will haunt you all the days of your life, and will, in the end, destroy you."

"Destroy me? Oh, come on," she said sarcastically. Then she was puzzled. "How did you know I was going to see Wisteria, the witch?"

He didn't answer her, but said, "I am telling you the truth. This is your chance, maybe your last chance, to turn from using this evil power, to renounce it and never return to it!"

Now she was beginning to get angry, and she wanted him to know it. "I don't wait around for things to happen, mister—I make 'em happen. I'm not some young kid! No, sir. Not me! I can take care of myself. This girl knows what she wants, and I find out how to get it," she announced stubbornly.

"Yes, I know you are very far from being a kid. As a matter of fact, you're not very young anymore are you?" He went on ignoring the anger appearing on her face. "Powers of darkness do not give anything to anyone for nothing. The payment is high; the cost is your very soul."

Karess was furious now, and she began to walk toward him, pointing her shoe. Suddenly, she stepped on something. "Ouch! Ooh," she moaned as she looked down to see her toe had a small cut. "Now look what you made me do," she cried. "I'm bleeding and it's all your—" But as she looked up again, the man and his donkey were gone.

"What—am I seeing things now?" she asked herself. Then she heard a voice out of nowhere, which seemed to resonate and fill up the whole forest.

"I have told you the truth today, and you still have time to turn back, but the choice is yours, alone, to decide."

Karess spun around, looking all over to see where he went, but nothing. Then she jumped back as a big shadow flew over her head. "Oh, my!" she said. "Whatever in this world is going on? Turn back? Powers of darkness," her head whirled, but then after thinking about it, she shrugged. *It was probably that old witch playing a trick on me*, she thought, and laughed it off nervously. Karess walked on. An eerie feeling crept over her as she finally spotted the witch's house.[11]

As she came to the small dark house, she knocked on the door. Nothing. She had to admit to herself there was a feeling of evil here, but she had her youth potion to think about. It would be impossible to give that up. Even she didn't know how old she actually was anymore, and she didn't let herself think about it. All that mattered was that she still looked very young and very glamorous, and she was determined to keep it that way.

Slowly, Karess opened the door, and it creaked as she entered. Crystals of every size and shape chimed and dangled and clinked together in a haunting way. She looked around the witch's room. There were jars filled with fluid, and inside were dead frogs with their mouths open and their eyes bulging out at her. Some jars were filled with just eyeballs with red threads that floated in the liquid. Weeds and herbs were hung up everywhere. There were locks of hair and small rag dolls with little pins stuck into them in strange places. Also, she noticed dried-up claws and feet, from different types of animals, hung from the ceiling on strings. "Oh, I don't even want to think about where she gets all this gross and ghastly stuff, ew! But she sure enough has just about every kind of concoction one would need to do just about anything," she whispered.

---

[11] Santana. "Black Magic Woman"

Rah, rah! The black raven screamed as the door suddenly slammed shut behind her.

"Huh!" cried Karess. Her heart began to pound wildly, and she was ready to run out the door when suddenly a huge, black bird came out of nowhere, flying over her head and landing on the door as if to stop her from leaving.

"Wisteria!" Karess called out frantically.

Rah! The bird screeched at her even louder.

Karess began to panic. "Let me out!" she cried, turning back to the door.

Rah! Rah! The black bird flapped about her.

"Wisteria! Wisteria!" Cried Karess, then she yelled to the big, black raven. "Shoo! Let me out! Shoo!" The bird fluttered closer to her and Karess jumped back from the door.

"Oh now, what is all this commotion about?" said Wisteria as she entered the room.

Karess put her hand on her chest. She was out of breath from her heart beating so fast. She gasped in between breaths, "Wisteria—that bird—oh my!"

Wisteria walked right past the bird and grabbed the old door knob. "Get out," she commanded. "You and your brother, Brutus, take off!" She yelled as she shooed the bird, and then the other flew out of nowhere and out the door. Wisteria slammed the door behind them. Turning back to Karess, she said, "Oh, dear, I am sorry about my little pets frightening you like that. Sit down, dear," she said as she offered her a chair.

"Now, what do you need today?" Wisteria asked.

Karess looked up at her. Gathering herself, she noticed that the witch wore her red hair loosely and wildly. It was thick, and had long waves that drooped and swayed past her waist. *Well, she still looks young and strangely pretty, except for her old, grey eyes,* Karess thought. As she took a deep breath, she began to get down to business. "I need a love potion," she announced.

"Oh, yes!" said the witch. "Of course, you need a love potion," she repeated. "And, dear, did you remember this time to bring something that belonged to the lucky man you want the potion for?"

Karess reached into her bag and pulled out a cotton handkerchief she had taken from Calvin's room and handed it to the witch proudly.

Wisteria brought out her crystal ball and put it onto the small, round table. She chanted a few words Karess could not understand as she watched the woman rub Calvin's handkerchief on the magic ball.

"Ah, yes," said Wisteria. "He's beginning to come into view," she announced. "Handsome young thing, isn't he?" she asked, not waiting for an answer. Then suddenly the witch leaned back, then peered closer to inspect the image in the ball, and said as she shook her head, "Oh, no, no, no, no! This won't do!"

"What?" asked Karess.

"Now, I hate to be the one to tell you this, but no potion is going to work on him, dear!"

"What?" she cried. "Why?"

Wisteria looked deep into the crystal ball. "Because he is covered!" she announced. "Covered by the light. See, look for yourself."

Karess squinted her eyes as she leaned into the ball. "Oh, I don't see a thing!" she said, getting annoyed with the witch. Everything was going wrong for her today, and she was at her wits end!

"The light, dear—the light around him—he's protected, get it? He is covered!"

"*Covered my butt!*" exclaimed Karess, who was at the end of her patience with the whole situation. "Make me the potion! Why, I've never heard of such a thing! You must be looking at too many crystals—I can't see anything!" Karess reached into her red bag and pulled out a thick wad of bills. "How about this!" she smirked, waving the money. "Will this uncover him?"

The witch smiled. "Whatever you want, dear. I'll make you the potion, dear. You just relax while I go behind the counter and mix you up the best love potion I can find."

"That sounds good," Karess nodded. "And make it a strong one!"

All was quiet while Wisteria brought out her thick, old, dusty book and began mixing her brew. Karess listened closely as the witch began muttering a mixture of horrible sounding things. She heard her mumble, "Three dead legs of a half-eaten caterpillar, and five drops of black juice from a bat's wing."

Suddenly, the door opened by itself with a huge gust of wind. In flew the two black birds. One of them flew across the room, and the other landed right on Wisteria's shoulder.

"Oh, Blacky!" laughed Wisteria. "Do you two ever leave Mumsy alone?"

Karess sat there, beginning to get very uncomfortable. She put her hand on her chest, and then the bird screeched as it flared out its black wings and stared at her with his beady black eyes.

"*Rah! Rah!* See the truth! See the truth!" screamed the bird.

Karess jumped in her chair. As Wisteria began to turn her head, Karess saw, for one split second, a skull and the half-eaten, worm-infested face of Wisteria. Then the witch instantly changed back into herself.

"Oh, help, somebody!" Cried Karess.

"What, dear? What is it now?" asked the witch, looking like herself again. "Oh, I know it's you two! Brutus!" she yelled. "You and Blacky, go outside like I told you to! Go fly around and cause trouble somewhere else for a while. Leave poor Karess alone!" she ordered as she shooed them away again.

Karess kept her head bent down, afraid of what she would see if she looked up. "Is it almost ready?" she asked, her voice becoming shaky.

Wisteria nodded to her. "But first we must add the real potent stuff! A spark of volcano, *poof!*" she chanted as the liquid sparked and crackled while Wisteria began to laugh. Wisteria cautiously put the brew into a special bottle as she reminded her of the instructions. "Don't forget, dear. Rub the mixture on your lips, and then you must kiss him within six minutes, and that's it."

Karess smiled as she handed the bills to the witch. "Believe me," she announced, "I won't forget that part."

Karess grabbed the potion and just about flew out the door. She limped with one shoe on and one shoe off through the dark woods. "This has been far too much work for a little ol' gal like me. I mean, I have just had enough!" she told herself as she tried to push the thoughts of men on donkeys and worm-eaten skulls out of her mind. "Ew!" she said out loud, "and those ugly, black ravens! Oh, it has been a terrible day! My shoe. My heart! It's been far too terrible a day for a pretty, young thing like me!"

Then she began to think about Calvin, and a smile returned to her face as she thought of him. "Soon he will be mine, because I know how to get exactly what I want, and then it will have all been worth it!" she said. Her eyes began to mist and flutter as she made the decision of exactly when and where and how she would give the magic kiss to Calvin Bella. She had to plan it all out to make sure it all went just the way she wanted. She swooned at the thought of putting her creamy lips on his, and giving him a long, breathy kiss, and she let out a long sigh as she dreamed of the moment he would be hers.

9
The Dance

Usually, the job at the factory went quickly for Calvin, but today was the day he was going to meet Crystalina. It was thinking about her that made the time go by so very slowly, and he thought three o'clock would never come.

After stopping at his suite to change, he went over to meet her. Along the way, he passed Dredge, the paper boy, who was shouting about the end of freedom for all people, and adding, "I knew this would happen someday!"

"Well, maybe it will," Calvin thought. But not today, not on this afternoon, the one he would spend with Crystalina.

He arrived at the candy store promptly at three, and she was just walking toward the door.

"Hello," he said, almost bumping into her.

"Hi. You're right on time!" she said.

The first place she led him to was the meadow, where there were fields of flowers and blooming trees. As they grazed through the lovely meadow, the aroma of the flowers filled the air. Calvin told her he had never seen so many things in bloom all at once. She told him that it was like that all the time.

"We have the four seasons here all year round. At least that's what other people have told me. I can't imagine it being any other way. It's always spring here in the meadow and in the Village, and as we walk farther toward the hidden falls, it will be summer."

"You're kidding!" Calvin exclaimed. "I don't think that this happens anywhere else in the world!"

Crystalina smiled, and he noticed she had a small dimple on one side of her cheek, enhancing her beautiful smile and her white teeth. "Yes, it's quite true. Up at the top of the mountain, it is always winter. We go sleighing up there quite a bit, and you must have noticed that, when you came into the Village, it was autumn." She suddenly ran toward a tree. "Here!" she said, laughing as she threw him a huge, ripe peach she picked from the tree.

Calvin caught the peach and said, "Hey, thanks. I guess you could never go hungry in Morningstar."

He followed her as she led the way through a path, and it was true; he could feel the air getting warmer and more humid, like a hot summer day. He saw there was a small clearing up ahead. He noticed an archway made of tall, thin trees, and as they stepped through, they walked onto a gazebo that was made out of trees, and covering the top was a natural grass that served as the roof. They looked out onto the gently flowing blue water that was enclosed with a high wall of rock with small waterfalls flowing into the center.

"Ah, Crystalina! It's more than I ever could have imagined or even dreamed it would be," he said. Then he looked at her, his eyes lingering on her pretty face, and thought to himself, but didn't dare say it. "And so are you."

They watched as three small waterfalls poured into the turquoise quarry. He marveled at the huge, rocky walls and the lush, tropical foliage, as well as all the huge flowers. It was as though the water filled the quarry, then overflowed, spilling gently over the lower side of the wall.

Red, pink, salmon, and lavender flowers were everywhere, but he decided it was the perfumed, giant-sized, white gardenia that he would pick and put in her hair. She smiled as they stood staring at the breathtaking sights. Then, suddenly, he heard her say, "Hey, look!"

Calvin looked at her, and there she was, up on a tall rock, holding a vine that connected to a huge tree overhead. "Wow!" he said.

"We can swing over to the other side of the quarry if you want to," she offered eagerly.

Calvin nodded and climbed the rock. Then, putting one arm around her and holding the vine with the other, he pushed off the rock, and they flew through the air together, across the crystal-clear quarry, and leapt off on the other side.

"Wow. That seems all I can ever say since I got here. It's all amazing, breathtaking, and more than I ever could have imagined!" Calvin said again, looking at

Crystalina, watching her as she laughed, her face flushed from the thrill.

They walked through the summer gardens for hours and headed back when it was dark. Calvin walked her to her front door and asked if he could see her again.

"Oh, I'd love to," she answered softly. "I'll tell you what: I have a horse called Shuga, and we could take him out next time, and I could really give you a thorough tour. And, if you want, we could even swim in the falls too."

"That sounds so fantastic! I'm counting the hours until we can go," he answered. They decided they would meet the same time the next day and Calvin was literally counting the minutes.

Calvin ran to Hedda's on his lunch break, and told him he was going with Crystalina to see the sights. "I'll buy everything you think she'll like, Hedda!"

Hedda was right on it, explaining the ingredients and giving Calvin a sample of all his great food. He even had a picnic basket he packed for him.

"So, you're actually going out with Crystalina, huh?" Hedda said in a surprised tone.

"Yes, but why do you seem so surprised?" asked Calvin.

"Well, you know, man, it's all really good. It's just that I've known her since she was born, and I've never seen her give any of the guys around here any attention, although many of them would love to get her attention, especially Dapper Snip. But she never seemed interested in them. She just hangs out with her friends. That is, until you came along, Cal."

Calvin was flattered, but he wasn't so glad to hear that his boss's son had liked her. "Oh, well," he said. "I'll take that as the best compliment I have ever gotten!"

"Hey, man, and you should!" agreed Hedda. "Anyway, how do you like living in the Village so far?"

"Hedda, I am so happy here. It's like, I just can't even say it in words. It's more than I ever dreamed."

"Glad to hear it, buddy!" Hedda said happily as he handed Calvin full basket of his luscious foods. "No worries, man. I got you. You just have a great time today, and say 'hi' to Crystalina for me."

"Will do, Hedda! Thanks!" Calvin said, eager to get going.

"And hey, Cal," said Hedda. "Keep me on the snap!"

"You got it! What's the snap?" asked Calvin, perplexed.

Hedda chuckled. "You gotta learn my lingo. The snap," he repeated. "Keep me posted."

"You know it!" Calvin said, then he rushed out the door and back to work.

Finally, he was with her again. They rode the white horse together, traveling through the meadows of spring, down the paths into summer, and delighted in the cool breezes of autumn. Then, spinning around again, they went back to the meadow where there was a long, lazy willow tree, and Calvin spread out a blanket underneath it and began to unpack the picnic basket he had brought for them.

They sat down and he thought, *I have so much I want to say, but is this the right time? Maybe it's too soon.* He looked at her, her long dark hair, and her deep green eyes, and then he heard her melodic voice.

She said, "So, Calvin, tell me about your family and where you come from."

They talked for a long time while they ate all of Hedda's delicious goodies. He confided in her about his mother and father and even Mrs. Tag. She was very sympathetic, especially when he told her of his mother's death and how much he missed her, even to this very day.

"But, you know, Crystalina, since I've come to Morningstar, I feel like I've been given a new life. I mean, before I felt like I wasn't really living. I loved my family, but, I mean, it just seemed all wrong, like something was missing, and then coming here and especially meeting you…"

She smiled and he noticed her eyes seemed to light up. Above them, perched on a branch, were five, little white lovebirds that they did not even know were there.[12] The little white lovebirds watched them and talked to each other, saying what a lovely couple they made, so

---

[12] Bloodstone. "Natural High"

they began to sing for them and actually did a little performance for the couple in the air.

Day after day they spent together, swimming in the falls and riding the horse through the meadows. They told each other their stories from the past and ate picnic lunches. They even swung from the vine and dove into the crystal clear waters of the quarry. It was all so perfect, so lovely, that it hardly seemed real.

Later that evening, Crystalina remembered she told Calvin that she would meet him at the dance the following night. Stacey had stopped by earlier and Crystalina had told her everything that had been happening. Then she told Stacey that in some ways she had never been so happy and elated, and in other ways she had never felt so uneasy, so unsettled. Stacey had said that it was easy to figure out why she felt that way.

"Why?" Crystalina asked anxiously.

"Don't you know?" Stacey asked, but could see from the look on her face that she didn't know at all. "Crystalina," she paused, "you're in love!"

All that night, Crystalina worried over what Stacey had told her that day. For the first time and the only time, she was in love. Now she was worrying herself sick wondering if Calvin felt the same way. *How could I tell?* she thought. *And what in the world will I do if he doesn't feel the same way?* These thoughts filled her head all night long. The next day, she could not bring herself to eat anything, and her mood was governed by her thoughts that swung back and forth between deciding she was sure he felt the same way as she did and being totally convinced that he was new in town and he just needed to get to know the place and the people a little better; that she was just a friend to him, someone he liked who could show him around.

"Oh, no!" she said out loud to herself. *How?* She wondered. *How did a person I've known such a short time totally take over my life?*

Karess sat at her vanity in her elaborate suite and pulled the brush through her blonde hair in long strokes. Her thoughts were of Calvin as she dreamed of a life with him at her side. The more she thought of him, the more eager she was to have him. Then, suddenly, she slammed the brush down as she remembered watching him all week long run in and out of the Inn, only to go off with Crystalina every spare second the man had. The only thing he had said to her all week was, "Do people really have Itchy's laundry clean their clothes?"

Karess answered him in her sweetest voice, "Why, they sure enough do, pumpkin," and then fumed with anger all day after he had thanked her and walked out the door. "Probably to see her again!" she seethed.

She can't hold a candle to me! Karess thought. *After all, I am a woman, and she is merely a girl! Imagine, I have to go and get a potion and put myself through all that trouble and expense, and he goes off with her! Well, that young man needs to learn a thing or two about good taste and havin' a real woman! Tsk, tsk!* Yet, she still could not understand why Calvin had paid so little attention to her and so much attention to Crystalina. "Why not me?" She asked, storming off. "Why not *me*?" she repeated as she went down the stairs.[13]

Almost every young person who lived in the Village was going to the dance that night. The whole community had been preparing for it for months. It was to be held at Titi's Tango Hut; a huge dancing arena that was indoors, but there were also tables set up outside around a dance floor under the stars. Uncle Peter's band would be performing, and they were having a surprise singer.

Everyone was excited except for Dredge, the paperboy, who kept bringing up everything he could think of to worry about. He announced that "the government was building bombs, and how could the people just go on dancing?" He also was concerned that there were many accidents that happened on dance floors anyway, and, also, that staying up late at night lowered your chances of fighting off sickness and disease. But when someone asked him where he was going to be that night, he told him, "Oh, at the dance, of course!"

Calvin had stopped by the lollipop shop in the morning just to say "hello" to Crystalina and also to tell her that he was looking forward to meeting her at the dance.

---

[13] The Judds. "Why Not Me"

The night had finally arrived, and everyone was buzzing from the anticipation of the dance. Everything was ready as Hedda brought in his delectable delights of literally hundreds of assorted pastries that he had handmade and designed. As he displayed them on the lovely decorated tables, he announced, "Everything is fresh! Fresh, the finest, and I made it all myself! The freshest food that can be found!"

Carlton and his wife, Feather, prepared a punch made from all the ripe, plucked fruits that grew wild in Morningstar. Uncle Peter's band was setting up and fine-tuning all their instruments as Titi and some friends put up the last of the lavish decorations. It was a beautiful night in the spring gardens of Morningstar Village, and, like every night in Morningstar, they all knew the weather would be perfect. Finally, the time had arrived.

The minute Calvin walked in the door of the dance, he spotted Hedda over by the pastry table and went to chat with him. As he walked, his eyes peered throughout the room, looking for Crystalina. The moment he walked up, Hedda said to him, "Hey, Cal, you're lookin' sharp, buddy!" and then added, "I haven't seen Crystalina come in yet, though."

Calvin smiled at the way Hedda knew exactly what he was thinking about, even before he said anything to him. He gazed around the room every couple of seconds, and he spotted Karess in a hot pink, lavishly silken gown with what looked to be a long, thin, white, furry thing she was waving at everyone as she said her hellos. As he looked again toward the front entrance door, he saw the Snip Trips coming in side by side. Their hair was done up—way up—about two feet on top of their heads in a cone shape, resembling three big beehives. They spotted him right away and began to run toward him with Bully at their side adjusting their paper gowns as they went.

"Calvin, Oh Calvin!" they yelled.

"Hi girls!" he answered, smiling. "You all look very festive."

They giggled and batted their eyelashes. "You look very handsome too," they said as they proceeded to introduce him to Bully, explaining that she was the dress designer.

"Oh, well, you're very talented," Calvin said, while looking at the dresses.

"Oh, I just love doing it," exclaimed Bully proudly. "And the girls just show off my designs so well, they're the perfect models!"

Calvin nodded and was about to say something when Beaky interrupted and said, "Oh Calvin, here comes our brother, Dapper. Have you met him yet?" Calvin told them he hadn't as he watched the young man walk up to his sisters. "Calvin, we would like you to meet our brother, Dapper Snip."

Calvin immediately offered him his hand, and Dapper shook it. "Hey, good to meet ya. Heard you work for my pop." Calvin nodded politely. "Yeah, well, I'll be joining you soon, or at least that's what Pop tells me," he said, laughing. Then he turned back to his sisters. "What are you girls wearing anyway?" Before they answered, he said, "And your hair looks like the top of Morningstar Mountain. Here let's take a jump off!" he teased, laughing hysterically, but before he could get out another remark, the three triplets started yelling at him and batting at him. No one could understand a word, because the three of them were yelling all at once.

"Yeah, yeah!" cried Dapper as he swatted back at them. "Hey, can't ya take a joke? Hey! Hey! Watch the merchandise," he exclaimed as he adjusted his suit jacket. "Well, Calvin, girls, this is my cue to take off. See yas later!" and he sped off quickly through the room, waving and laughing as he went.

"Oh, that spoiled brat!" cried Birdy.

"Yeah!" agreed Beaky and Swobbie.

"Wait 'til we get home and tell Daddy!" cried Swobbie. "How dare he say anything about the way I look? He doesn't know the latest style in Europe like we do!" she added. And with that, all three girls sauntered off to the ladies room looking quite indignant.

The lights began to dim as the candles were lit all around the room. Calvin could see that the doors were open on one side of the room, which led out to more tables with lit candles that glowed softly everywhere under the moonlit night. Up on the stage, the curtains were still tightly drawn, and he didn't know when the band would start to play. The room was beginning to really fill up with people dressed in their best clothes, and he sipped his punch and watched intently as each person walked in. He waited for the moment when he would see her. He spotted a waiter who offered him a pastry, but he declined politely and the waiter took his empty glass.

He started toward the door and was halfway there when he saw Stacey walk in, hesitating. He then saw Suey, then Kell, then—he stopped and stood, waiting. Nothing.

Puzzled, he stepped closer, and then, there she stood in the doorway. He drew in his breath and almost felt light-headed at the very sight of her. *She is the most beautiful girl I have ever seen,* he thought, and then quickly thanked God for letting him come here to this unbelievable place and thanked him, most of all, for her.

Crystalina was draped in a pale lavender shade of velvet, her long, dark, wispy curls in and around her face and flowing down her back.

He walked toward her then, and offered her his hand. She took it, and he leaned in and kissed her lightly on the cheek, and as he did, he whispered in her ear, "I was counting the seconds until you got here." Then, stepping back he looked at her, he smiled. "You are so lovely," he told her. She smiled back at him, holding on to the ticklish chill that ran right down her back when he had softly whispered in her ear.

They heard the sound of music and the curtains began to part as the people rushed toward the dance floor.

"Ladies and Gentlemen, we would like to introduce our special guest singer tonight that will be accompanied by Uncle Peter's all time band! Are you ready?" the announcer asked as the crowd shouted back to him.

"Yeah!"

"Will you all join me in welcoming Ms. Destiny Ravis!" he shouted as Destiny came onto the stage singing her heart out. The crowd cheered and clapped with great glee for the singer as she began her song. Calvin wasted no time and asked Crystalina to dance. She nodded and he led the way to the dance floor. Under the soft candlelight, he turned and reached for her.

They melted into each other's arms and started to move gently together with the rhythm of the song.[14] The night suddenly had such a magical feeling as the room filled with music, and he held her close. As he listened to the words of the singer, he felt as if she were singing all the things he had been waiting for the right time to say to Crystalina.

It seemed that they both forgot that other people were even in the room with them. As he drew her closer, they glided together under the moon. He could smell her perfume, and everything about her made him want to kiss her right there. Then, suddenly, Calvin felt a quick tug on his arm. Startled, he turned to look, and it was Karess telling him to come with her quickly, for just

[14] Orpheus. "Can't Find the Time"

a moment, as she pulled him away from Crystalina—Calvin was stunned out of the enchanted moment he was having with her.

"Just for one little ol' minute. There is just one good friend of mine that's been waitin' forever to meet you!"

Calvin looked up at Crystalina, who grinned and gave a quick nod as if to say she understood that he needed to be polite. He shrugged back at her and gave his eyes a little roll as Karess dragged him across the room with her white feathered thing flying into his face.

"Now, honey, you just have to meet these people. It's for your very own good, since you'll be livin' here now, *tsk, tsk*." She winked at him as she walked up to two girls in the corner, one standing behind the other leaning her head off to one side, giving them the appearance of having two heads.

"Now, this, here, is Marla Murmur and Rita Bobita!" announced Karess. Both girls looked him up and down, and both were chewing gum and blowing bubbles, as Marla put her hand on one hip and began bobbing up and down leaning more on one leg.

"Nice to meet you," Calvin said politely and added, "are you enjoying the dance?"

"*Enjoying* the dance," Marla exclaimed. "Are you *kidding*? *Who* do you think put up most of these decorations?" she cried. "Me and Rita, that's who! And we had to rush down to pick up our dresses, and they weren't even ready! Why, she was still sewing them, and then we schlepped back here to clean up, and then schlepped back to get the dresses and home to get *ready,* and you just can't imagine how we *schlepped* all day long!"

Rita nodded her head out from behind her friend's neck as Marla roared on, and Rita kept agreeing and added, as she chewed her gum, "Yup, we *schlepped!*"

Then Marla suddenly put her hand up in front of Calvin's face, as if to make a big stop sign, and announced, "Don't talk! *You* don't know what *we* have *been* through trying to get ready for this dance!"

"Yeah!" Rita nodded and chewed onward. "You don't know what we've been through!"

"I don't even think I could *possibly* dance now!" cried Marla.

"Yeah," Rita nodded. "She can't dance now!"

Calvin was speechless and did not know what to say, even if they ever allowed him to get a word in. Then, Karess appeared again, out of nowhere.

He did not know that while he was talking, Karess had run over to tell the girls, especially Crystalina, how Calvin had been asking her to introduce him to Marla ever since the moment he had moved to Morningstar, and that he was thrilled to be getting to know all the girls in town. She went on to say that he asked her to show him around quite a few times, but, being a business woman, she was much too busy to be sightseeing. Then, she said, directly to Crystalina, that it was sure enough nice of her to offer to show Calvin around, but the other girls would be happy to show him around too. Karess could see by Crystalina's expression that she was shocked and looking upset, like she was going to cry. Karess then went off to the ladies' room and covered her shiny, red lips with the oily potion and prepared to finish her dirty, little deed. She had less than six minutes left to make it happen.

"Come on, sweetie," Karess said, dragging Calvin by the arm again.

"Listen, Karess. I told Crystalina—"

Karess turned back to him quickly. "Oh, sweetie, I just want you to have the proper welcome is all." She stopped dragging him and pulled him quickly into her, knowing Crystalina could see them clearly now, and then she gave him a hard, tight, full kiss on the mouth before Calvin could move out of her grip.

Calvin was stunned, and before he had a chance to say anything, she said, "Now, you just have yourself a great ol' time here tonight! *Tsk, tsk*." She winked and strolled off as quickly as she had appeared.

Calvin pulled himself together and began to look for Crystalina. After searching the whole place in and outside, he found Stacey.

"Stacey," he called after her. "Have you seen Crystalina?"

"Last time I saw her, she was waiting for you."

Calvin searched the room again, and then began to look and ask anyone who may have seen her. He made his way through the crowd again and toward the front door. He stepped outside and saw the doorman and he quickly described the dark haired girl with the lavender dress, asking him if he'd seen her.

"Yup," he said pointing, "I watched her run up that hill and into the night, and I thought it was strange that she was all alone."

Calvin immediately called out her name. "Crystalina!" he shouted into the night. He began to run as he looked back at the doorman, asking again, "This way?"

The doorman nodded, and Calvin ran down the deserted streets, wondering why on earth she would leave him like that. *Where did she go?*

He ran to the only place he thought she would go at night, and that was to her own home. He stopped in front of her house. All seemed quiet, but before going on up to the porch, he tried to catch his breath. Gathering his thoughts, he went up and knocked on the door. No answer. He knocked again and again.

Finally, her mother Rose, who he had met only briefly, came to the door. She looked at him, and before he had a chance to say anything to her, she announced, "My daughter came home early and was upset. She has gone to her room and does not want to be disturbed. Goodnight, sir!" and she shut the door firmly in his face.

Calvin walked along the lonely streets and felt almost numb. He could not understand what had happened. He remembered the song, and could hear the music still playing in his ears as he walked alone. He thought of the words he had so longed to say to her tonight, and now? He couldn't understand. Then he thought of Karess's kiss and wondered if that was what had upset her. "She *must* know I have no interest in Karess," he said to himself.

When he got back to his room at the Inn, he found the place empty, and he was relieved for that. There was no way he could even hold a conversation about anything, not after he held all his happiness within his arms and then watched it all disappear into the night.

He tossed and turned, but could not fall asleep. Over and over, he kept wondering *why?* He tried to hold onto the hope that maybe tomorrow she would see him, and he could find out what happened.

But the next day came and went, and she would not see him or talk to him, and he spent most of the night awake again.

Meanwhile, Karess began to realize that the witch might have been right. The potion hadn't done a thing to Calvin. It seemed he had not even seen her, even though he walked right past her that very morning and didn't even say one word. But before she despaired, she decided to give it a couple more days to kick in. After all, she never asked Wisteria how long it took to do its magic.

Days turned into weeks, and every time Calvin tried to see Chrystalina, the door was shut in his face. She had not even worked at the lollipop shop. Finally, one afternoon, he ran into Stacey. In a desperate attempt to reach Crystalina, he asked Stacey if she would possibly try to talk to her for him; give him just one chance to explain.

"I don't know, Calvin," answered Stacey uncomfortably.

Calvin looked down. "Do you know why she won't see me?"

"Listen, Calvin, I hate to be the one to tell you this, but Crystalina is dating Dapper now. Dapper Snip."

Calvin felt his head begin to spin. "Oh," he said as he tried to remain standing. "Is it serious?" he gulped.

"Well, to be honest, I keep asking her the same thing, but she says that he is the one she wants and that she is happy with him. Other than that, she hasn't said anything else about the dance or you, and, at this point, I just want my friend to be happy." She looked at him sympathetically. "I am sorry Calvin."

"Hey, don't be sorry. You're right; if she's happy, that's what matters," he told her. He forced a smile and walked on. He didn't really know where he was going, but ended up at the waterfall where he had first seen her.

Well, that's it, he thought. *It's over and I'll never have the one girl I will ever love.* Calvin felt his heart breaking. How, he wondered, could he even begin to compete with the very popular and very rich Dapper Snip? He couldn't. He put his head in his hands. *I've lost her.*

Crystalina looked out her window, she heard someone calling her name. It was Dapper, yet again. She went down and sat on the porch swing with him. He talked on and on about his plans and what he was going to buy next. Then, suddenly, he tried to kiss her. She turned from him at first, but then he touched her face and slowly turned her back toward him and gently kissed her lips. He held his kiss for a long moment, and she felt tears welling up in her eyes and an aching lump beginning to form in her throat, knowing that when she opened her eyes she'd be looking at the wrong man.

"Dapper," she said choking back tears, "I'm a little tired tonight."

Dapper smiled. "Okay, but there's something I want you to think about. Don't answer yet though, just think it over."

"Well, what is it?" she asked.

"I want to marry you, Crystalina. Will you be my wife? Don't answer yet, but listen; I can give you a great life..." He smiled again as he plucked at her long dark curls. "Think about it, sleep on it, and I'll see you tomorrow at the park, like we said." He kissed her again quickly, smiled, turned, and left.

Crystalina sat there on the swing in shock. Never had she expected that. "What am I doing anyway?" she asked herself out loud. She thought, somehow, that if she went out with Dapper it would help her forget Calvin. After all, Dapper was fun, even if he was a spoiled brat, she reasoned. But, nothing worked. She was feeling worse each day. But every time she remembered what Karess had said, and then that kiss, she felt she was a fool for ever thinking that Calvin had cared for her. Now, here she was with Dapper Snip, who she would never really love, and now he wanted to marry her.

The next day, she had decided that she would meet Dapper, but she had to put an end to this right away.

She met him in the park that was in the center of the Village. They sat at a small table outside while Dapper ordered lunch. It was a warm weekend afternoon, and she realized it had been three weeks since the dance. Three weeks since she had seen Calvin.

"Well, did you think about my proposal?" asked Dapper.

"Yes, well, that's what I—"she stopped, then, as she noticed in the distance Calvin walking through the Village with Karess. She could see Karess was pawing him as they strode together down the sidewalk. Karess was talking or whispering into his ear and laughing.

All her anger and humiliation she'd suffered at the dance rose up inside her instantly. She'd felt like a fool. All the feelings from that terrible night rushed back and she heard herself suddenly blurt out, "Yes, Dapper, I will marry you!"

10
Can You Hear Me?

The talk about the biggest wedding that anyone had seen in years spread through the Village like wildfire. Everyone in the entire Village was to be invited to attend the marriage of Crystalina Devine and Dapper Snip. Crystalina's friends and family were all very excited for her. Biffer Snip was thrilled, and offered to spare no expense when it came to his only son's wedding.

Crystalina, on the other hand, was ready to flee the country. Since the moment she had accepted his proposal, she'd begun to try to think of ways to get out of it. Now she could have also created a potential problem for her parents, since Dapper's father was the one that owned their home. If she broke off her engagement, what would become of her parents' home? He could raise the rent and keep on raising it until they could no longer afford to stay there, or, worse, he could throw them out! He had kept the rent low for them all these years because he liked them. And she knew it would cause her Aunt Jayja a lot of embarrassment too. She was definitely in trouble now, and she decided that she had never acted so foolish or been so miserable in all her life. What had she done?

Calvin heard the news about the engagement from Karess, and when she told him, he thought he would drop down right then and there in front of her. It was all he could do to not pack up and go right back to his hometown. He barely spoke to anyone, and began working extra hours and then going right to bed.

He had written a letter weeks ago to Mrs. Tag, and finally had received word back from her, congratulating him on reaching Morningstar. She told him she would be praying for him every day and that she had faith he would do really well. *If she only knew*, thought Calvin.

He had also written to his stepmother to let her know his address in case she should want to reach him. He hadn't heard back from her and did not really expect to. *No,* he thought as he remembered her, *going back is not an option.*

One morning, he arrived at work early and Mr. Snip was already there, checking on business. Calvin greeted him. "Calvin," said Mr. Snip, "I'm glad you're here. I wanted to talk to you about your job. Have a seat."

Calvin sat in the chair Mr. Snip offered to him.

"Listen, my boy, you've been doing an excellent job, and one thing about me, I reward people if I like 'em. I've decided I like the way you work. So, I've been thinking of promoting you to assistant manager. It would mean more money and also I will include a very nice little house for you to live in." Snip announced. "I know you think that is most generous of me, but I am happy lately, exceptionally happy about my son's upcoming wedding to the beautiful Crystalina, who will become my wonderful daughter-in-law. Yes. Dapper did a good job, for once. This time I am proud of his decision. She is such a little gem," Snip said as he cleared his throat and grabbed a tissue to wipe his spectacles. "Anyway," he went on, "I am a businessman, and this position will require that you will have to work longer hours," Snip said as he studied Calvin's expression. "Well, are you up for the task?"

Calvin was up for anything that would keep him busy now, and he listened intently to his new responsibilities. He was very glad to hear about moving into his own house, but hearing him talk about Crystalina and the wedding felt like a knife to his heart, and he tried hard not to wince as Snip made his gleeful announcements.

Snip went over all that was required of him and announced that he could move into his new place over the weekend. "But, Calvin, there is not much in there for furniture, just a bed and a kitchen table and chairs. You'll have to take care of the rest of it yourself."

"Fair enough, Mr. Snip," Calvin said as he reached out to shake his hand.

Calvin moved into his little house in the Village that very weekend. Karess practically threw herself at his feet, begging him not to go. He thanked her for all her hospitality, but told her it was time.

He found the little place charming, but Snip had been right when he had told him it was sparse. So, Calvin began to make some furniture for his new home right away. He was glad, in a way, to be kept so busy; it took his mind off of Crystalina, at least for a few moments, anyway. Since that night that she had left him, he had been carrying with him this horribly empty feeling inside that he just couldn't get rid of, and he really did not have the slightest idea of what he could do to change anything.

When nothing seemed to help, Calvin would walk through the meadows of Morningstar, and often went to the quarry. In some ways, it made him feel worse to go there, because he would remember every little detail of the time he had spent with Crystalina. In other ways, it made him feel close to her again as he relived all the moments of joy he had shared with her, but eventually it would only lead him back to the fact that she was gone and engaged to marry someone else.

He was thinking just that, as he sat on the edge of the gazebo with his feet dangling in the cool blue water, when a small white bird landed on his hand. Calvin was surprised. He had never seen a wild bird that would fly right into your hand, and it was such a cute, little, fluffy white bird. He carefully moved his hand up and began to pet it with one finger, ever so gently. "Where did you come from?" he asked the bird. Within a moment, another bird just like it flew into his hand and just sat there, chirping and playing with its mate. Calvin watched with wonder as the two birds danced around, flew and fluttered, and then would land together, right back in his hand. "What a place this is," he said out loud, laughing. "I don't think anyone would even believe it me if I told them." Then, as the birds sat there in the palm of his hand, they began to touch and then swoon around each other, and Calvin had the strangest feeling that they were actually trying to say something to him.

Suddenly he recalled the first time he had seen Crystalina at the waterfall with her friends, how familiar she had seemed to him even though he knew he had never met her. Then he remembered the small, quiet voice that had spoken to his heart that first day, telling him, "Yes Calvin. She's the one."

He looked down at the little, innocent birds and remembered, too, the dream and what the angel had said to him. "When things look hopeless, he can do all things for the one who believes!"

And it was like a fire that's been put out by a fierce rain, yet a small ember still carries a spark, hidden in the center. So it was, at that moment inside Calvin's heart. The hope for a miracle was ignited within him. He didn't have any idea when, where, or how, but he believed that God had spoken that day at the water, that he had been led to this place. It was his destiny, and she was to be in his life, and somehow, someway, someday, he and Crystalina would be together again, and he vowed he would not let go of that belief, no matter how grim the situation appeared.

The next day after work, Calvin stopped in to see Hedda. He had to talk to someone, and he confided in Hedda his hopes about Crystalina.

"Hey, if you believe in it that strongly, you hold that faith, buddy, and I'm gonna be with ya on that too!" Hedda told him, not daring to say that Biffer had asked him to make the cake for his son's wedding.

Just then, they both turned to see Dredge walking through the door. He scuffled along and then stopped cold and stared at Calvin.

"Hey, aren't you the new guy that's moved into town?" asked Dredge. Hedda introduced them, and Dredge started to question Calvin. "So, since you've been out in the other part of the world more than most of us, tell me, have you witnessed any signs of *the end*?"

Calvin didn't really know what he meant so he repeated, "*The end?*" Then he thought about it for a second and said, "Oh—you mean the end of the world?"

Hedda interrupted, "Dredge, don't start! Have a seat and relax before I have to slap you out of it." Hedda pointed to the chair, half annoyed and half smiling.

"Hey, hey, I'm just watchin' for the signs," Dredge protested as he sat his small, thin body down in the chair.

"Good," said Hedda, "Keep watchin', but in the meantime, have a dreamcup that will keep your mouth busy."

Hedda handed Dredge the luscious-looking pastry puff and patted him on his shaved head.

"Yes," said Hedda to Calvin. "Dredge gets all the outside news and the inside info too," he said, rolling his eyes as he kneaded and twirled a ball of dough. "Right, Dredge?"

Dredge nodded as he stuffed his mouth. "Nobody cooks like you Hedda, I'll give ya that!" His full mouth mumbled as he licked the cream off each finger.

The door swung open again, and it was Dapper Snip. "Hey, pal!" he said to Calvin, jabbing him with his elbow as he walked past.

"What are ya cookin' up for me today, Heddy, ol' bud?" Dapper asked as he inspected the glass counter with all the delicious displays of food. No one uttered a sound, they just stood looking at him with wide eyes. "Hey, what is it, a funeral around here or what?" Dapper said chuckling. "Oh, I know," he said sarcastically to Calvin. "You're sore about losing Crystalina to me. Well, ya can't win 'em all, pal, right? But it is a huge loss, ain't it, Cal?" he elbowed him again. "There's more fish in the sea, but I got the best one for me!" He roared with laughter and headed toward the door. "Hey, Hedda!" he yelled back. "Pack me up a dozen dreamcups! I'll pick 'em up right before I go to get my fiancée. Ooh, I am counting the minutes until I see her. Hey, don't forget now, and no slacking! About an hour, have 'em ready."

The door swung shut as quickly as it had opened, and Hedda and Dredge stared at Calvin, and no one, not even Dredge, dared to say a word.

As much as Calvin had vowed to have faith, he found it next to impossible to stop visualizing Crystalina and Dapper together. The more he thought of it, the more furious he got. By later that evening, he was fuming mad. It was all he could do to not run down the street screaming, waving a big stick around, like he had with the hyenas. He was so upset, he was beside himself. He went to bed and it was just another night staring at the ceiling as the hours ticked by, and it was becoming clearer by the minute that there would be no sleeping for him again.

Someone, and Crystalina could not remember who, told her she had to go to Bully's to look at wedding gowns. The triplets and Stacey were with her, and they brought out one gown out after another, and Crystalina never saw any of them. Dapper had given her a huge emerald engagement ring that they were all admiring, and Crystalina had barely looked at that either. She tried to keep her mind off everything; Dapper, the wedding, her parents, Biffer Snip, and most of all, Calvin. She was just going through the motions. It was the fact that the four girls, Stacey, Kell, Suey, and she, were going sleighing the next day, which kept her going.

Somebody wrote down the name of a good coachman for her to contact that could chauffeur her and her bridesmaids to her wedding. She smiled politely and thanked her, but felt like asking, "And do you know anybody who could chauffeur me about a million miles from here?"

The following day, very late in the afternoon, Calvin was in his back yard working on a piece of furniture he was making when he heard banging. He went around to the front of the house and there was Stacey, pounding on his door.

"Stacey, what is it?" asked Calvin, seeing she was upset.

"Calvin! Oh, Calvin!" Stacey cried breathlessly.

"What is it? What's going on?" he asked again.

"It's Crystalina!" she said frantically, trying to catch her breath and steady herself.

"Tell me, what's wrong?" he asked urgently.

"Well, the four of us went sleighing up on the top of the mountain. Each of us had our own sleighs, you know, and we were taking turns going down the same trail and walking back up. Suey was on her way down, and Kell and I were walking back up. As we were heading up, both of us kept expecting to see Crystalina coming down after Suey but, we never saw her come down!" she choked. "She disappeared! We looked high and low. We called for her, but she is just gone!" Stacey began to cry. "Calvin, I'm so worried. There are cliffs up there and a storm was starting and we decided we had better run for help!" She paused trying to go on, "The first thing we did was to go get Dapper, you know, so he could go after her, but he told us there was *no way*! He told us that it was getting too dark, and, with a storm coming, he'd said he could *never find her!*" Stacey told him as she sobbed.

Calvin was half way in the house when he told her, "I know what to do! Try to stay calm, Stacey." Even though deep inside Calvin was frantic, he ran into the house and bundled up as best as he could, grabbed one of his lanterns, then, without another word, he was off racing toward the mountain with all of his might.

It seemed like it had taken forever for him to reach the top of the mountain. It was pitch black up there, and he had to stop and use the fire from the lantern to light a torch so that he could see. Hours had passed and he was desperately worried about Crystalina. He had tracked and followed tree-line paths in and out as he made his way up, calling her name over and over, but nothing. Soon he was at the top of the mountain, and he began to descend in a weaving pattern so that somehow, someway, he would find her. [15] "*Can you hear me, Crystalina*?" he called out again and again. All he heard was his own echo. It was snowing much harder now, and all the tracks from their sleighs were completely gone. Worse, his feet were beginning to sink into the mounting snow, and he knew it was only a matter of time before his freezing feet would be soaked.

---

[15] Electric Light Orchestra. "Believe Me Now"

As he approached the other side of the mountain, he stumbled upon something and fell flat on his face. As he got up to brush himself off, he stopped quickly in his tracks. Through the blaze of his torch he could see he was only inches away from falling off a huge cliff. He began to back away. *Another step and I would have fallen hundreds of feet to who knows where!* Then he thought of Crystalina. *Oh, no! Oh, please, God, no. She couldn't have fallen*—he stopped himself, he could not even think like that. With God's help, he would find her somehow, someway, and it had to be soon. He just had to keep searching.

He began to notice that the storm was getting worse. The wind was blowing harder, and his voice could barely be heard above the screeching of the whipping, windy snow. Back and forth, he had weaved his way around that mountain, calling her name. He could no longer keep the torch lit in the fierce winds. He could barely move his freezing hands and feet. He didn't even know where to look anymore. He feared that now he was going in circles. Half frozen, he held onto a tree and used it as a shield to keep him away from the frigid winds. He looked toward the sky. "Help me," he whispered in desperation as he waited, trying to think of what he could do. It was pitch black now, and the only light he had came from the moon.

"Hey, you!"

Calvin was startled and looked up toward the sky.

"No, it ain't him talkin' to ya! It's me, over here."

Calvin looked around and suddenly saw a small light flickering toward him. It was a short, little man with an extraordinarily long beard, carrying a lantern.

This can't be God, can it? Calvin asked himself.

"Come on, git on over here," the little man said, waving to him to come along, his voice, nasal-sounding and very annoyed.

Calvin didn't care who it was at that point, and ran toward him. "Sir," Calvin said, "I'm looking for a girl and—"

"Yup, yup, as if I didn't know who ya was lookin' fer! I know yer not up here pickin' daisies in this here snow storm!"

"You've seen her!" Calvin said hopefully.

"A'course I seen 'er. Follow me. What, did ya think I'm just out here on a stroll?" The little man led him down a path through the trees, down the steeper side of the mountain, and there, at the end of it all, was a small door. It seemed as if the house was built right into the mountain.

"Is she in there?" Calvin shrilled. "Is she?"

"A'course she is," the little man answered.

"Oh, thank God. Thank you, God!"

"Hey, don't thank him, thank me! Now, come on. Git going in dere, dang it, before we done freeze to death!"

Calvin ran into the little cabin and felt the warmth of a fire instantly. He looked across the little room and there she was, all blanketed up near the fire, asleep on a sofa, but more beautiful than ever. "Thank God," he whispered again.

The little man handed him a cup of something hot, and Calvin took it gratefully.

"Now, keep your trap down and let her rest a little while longer. She's got quite a bump on that perty head of 'ers."

"Is she alright?" Calvin asked, getting alarmed again.

"So, I look like a dern doctor now? Yap, yap, yap—geez, you people! I come all the way up here to git away from all this noise and jibber-jabber, and whats do I get? People falling down the mountain, landin' at my dang door, sick, hurt, half froze, or half dead!" The little man shook his head. "Ya know, I tell ya, it's always somethin' with you people!"

Calvin looked at him with an open mouth. "What happened to her?" he asked.

"Now, what the heck do I look like to ya, *the all-seeing eye*? Geez," he said shaking his head again. "As if this don't happen all the dang time! All I knows is I'm havin' a peaceful, quiet day, mindin' my own dang beeswax, and I hear a big thump and then a holler and then another thump! Then I says to myself, *self, forget yer peaceful, quiet day!* Then, I have to bundle myself up and trudge out into the snow and save someone else's dang life. Again!"

"Thank you for helping her. If it wasn't for you, well," he paused, "I don't even want to think about it." He stopped, looking over at her. "By the way, my name is Calvin, and I—"

"Save it," the old man said. "But—for the record, I'm Buxston Gizzard. But that don't mean we's gonna be friends or nothin'. *Geez.* I moved up here to get away from all them dang people and have my own place. Most of 'em all're greedy things anyway, with their greedy, little, wiggly fingers always reachin' out to take another buck, and always yappin'. Ya, yappin'!" he repeated. "Or chewin' on somethin', constantly crunchin', geez. Drives me bugs, all that chewin', yappin', and grabbin'. Who needs it? Then they trudge up here and I gotta save 'em! Then they wants to tell ya their whole life story! Who cares! I tell ya, there's no gittin' away from it."

"Well, Mr. Gizzard, if there's anything I can ever do to repay you, just say the word!" Calvin told him gratefully.

"When your little missy wakes up, you twos just skedaddle back down the mountain, but *don't tell no folks I's livin' up here*, ya hear?" He squinted his eyes toward Calvin.

"It's a deal," Calvin said as he walked quietly back over to Crystalina. He sat next to her, looking at her for hours. It felt so good just to be near her again. Finally, he fell asleep on the floor in front of the fire.

When first light came in the morning he looked over at her. She was still sleeping. "Crystalina," he whispered as he began to shake her gently.

After trying several times to wake her he walked up to Buxston and said nervously, "She won't wake up."

"I don't knows what to tell ya. She got quite a bump," he answered shaking his head, looking a bit concerned.

"I better take her down the mountain and get her to a doctor," Calvin said, worried.

"You go ahead then, and keep her wrapped up tight in dat ol' blanket," he told him as he handed Calvin some hot liquid.

"Well thank you," Calvin said quietly as he headed out the door with her, still sleeping and wrapped in his arms. "You saved her life, and for that, I am forever grateful to you."

"Well now, I guess dat's why the Good Lord puts me here fer, anyhow! But, listen, you better git goin', but you be careful now and git your little legs down there safe, 'cause I ain't comin' to git ya again, now! You make sure you git 'er to a good doc., not no quick-talkin' quack, like most of 'em are, ya know," Buxston told him sternly, but Calvin could see in his eyes there was a warm, concerned smile.

Calvin walked carefully down the mountain, being sure to watch where he was going as he carried the sleeping Crystalina in his arms. He kept the blanket Buxston had given him tightly wrapped around her. He was becoming increasingly more worried by the minute, wondering if even a doctor would be able to wake her up.

11

Never, My Love

As Calvin neared the foot of the mountain, he could see a small crowd of people already gathered there. He could hear sighs and shouts of joy as he approached them. They began to applaud. Calvin noticed that Dapper was nowhere in sight.

Hedda walked toward him and took Crystalina from his arms as Stacey ran up to look at her.

"Good job, man," said Hedda.

"She won't wake up," Calvin said, shaking his head.

They hurried as they carried her home, and Rose rushed to open the door, looking frantic and exhausted. "Oh, thank God you found her!" cried Rose. "Is she hurt?"

"No—well, we don't know yet," Calvin said as he tried to explain what had happened.

Harry hobbled up to his daughter and then looked at Calvin, who was holding her. "Thank you, Calvin. Thank you so much for saving her and bringing our daughter back to us."

Calvin didn't say any more. He knew by the haunted look on their faces that they all knew there was something wrong, but no one knew why she wouldn't wake up. He carried her up the stairs and gently laid her on the bed, telling her parents that Stacey and Hedda had already gone to get the doctor.

When the doctor arrived, they each took turns pacing through the room downstairs as they waited to hear what he would say. It seemed like he was in there examining her forever. Finally, he came out and told them there was nothing anyone could do but wait.

Everyone just stared at him, astonished. But that is what Calvin did; he sat in the chair beside her bed and waited as another day and then another night passed.

Then more days passed, and Calvin remained at her bedside, staring at her, willing her to wake, whispering to her. Nothing. The doctor had come by every day, but by the fourth day, he told Rose and Harry that the longer she remained in the coma, the less chance there was of her waking up at all.

Rose could not keep herself from crying, and Harry was so worried that he had not uttered a word in days. Calvin felt truly sorry for them.

"Mrs. Devine," said Calvin, but she didn't answer right away.

"Oh, Calvin. I'm sorry, dear. I was just lost in my thoughts. You know, I never apologized to you for how I treated you when you were trying to—"

Calvin put his hand up and shook his head. "No need to say anything. I understand completely. I just wanted to talk a minute and to say that I really feel that she will be all right. I can't really say how I know, but I know she will wake up. I mean, don't get me wrong, I am very worried, but I believe she'll come back to us. She just has to."

Rose stared at him for a long moment. "These flowers came from Dapper the other day. And I was just thinking, right before you walked into the room; it's because of him. Dapper, I mean."

Calvin looked puzzled.

"She doesn't really want to marry him! I could see it in her eyes. I don't know what happened that night at the dance, but I know this, Calvin: it's you that she wants. Don't you see? That's why she hasn't woken yet. She can't stand to face the fact that she's engaged to the wrong man. And you know what, Calvin? I agree with her!" Then Rose turned to Harry, "I'm right about this, aren't I, Harry?"

"Yes, you definitely are right," answered Harry, who spoke for the first time in days. "And I agree that Calvin is the far better choice. After all, he saved her life. Why, that Dapper just left her up there. Maybe he had his reasons, but action speaks louder then… flowers!"

Calvin watched as Rose whizzed by him and up the stairs to Crystalina's room. Both he and Harry followed her.

They could hear Rose talking to her as they walked in.

"Now, you listen, my darling. You are not going to marry Dapper. Your father and I know full well he is not right for you, and we would be terribly unhappy to see you marry him. So you're not to worry about a single thing. We'll take care of the Snips. But Crystalina, your father and I are waiting for you to come back to us..." She began to sob. "That is all we care about, my darling sweetheart. And there is someone else who needs you just as much as we do, so come back, sweetheart, come back...." Her mother sobbed as she stroked and so very delicately placed Crystalina's hair.

Calvin stayed in the chair beside her bed. Later that evening, he touched her hand, and then he kissed it. "Crystalina," he whispered. "I don't really know if you can hear me or not, but I'm going to say what I should have said to you before, because it's the truth. I love you, I've always loved you." He paused, watching her motionless expression. "Just being near you, hearing your voice, makes me feel like I'm really living life again. It makes me feel that everything is right, finally, the way it was meant to be. Without you, Crystalina, I am only half alive." He touched her cheek gently. "Sleep as long as you must, my love."

The next morning there was no change in her. He looked at her for a long time and she seemed to be getting paler. He was just walking out the doorway when he heard her whisper.

"Calvin?"

He froze for a minute, almost afraid to turn, afraid he had imagined hearing her voice. Turning to her slowly, he saw her looking up at him, and she was awake!

"Crystalina," he said softly, joyfully. "You've come back!"

The doctor came and examined her again and told them that he didn't see anything wrong with her, and that it would just take a few days to get her strength back.

Calvin sat with her and told her what had happened and where he found her, and even told her about Buxston Gizzard, and they both laughed but were so thankful to him.

Rose and Harry came in and as they talked they insisted that she break it off with Dapper. "You know, that's the funny thing; the first thing I thought of when I woke was that I was definitely not going to marry Dapper!" Crystalina told them it was a moment of complete clarity.

"He was never for you!" said her mother, nodding her head in agreement. "I could see it in your eyes! Anyway, look at this one here," she announced, pointing to Calvin, who stood beside them. "Why, he looks like some kind of a Greek God, doesn't he?" She didn't wait for an answer but yelled out, "Harry—! Doesn't Calvin look like a Greek God?"

"He certainly does," answered Harry, "and a brave one too!"

They all made a toast to Crystalina's health. Then Calvin told them that he had to leave, but would be back the next afternoon to check on her.

Rose said, "Wait, Calvin, why don't you take the horse, and you can bring her back when you come tomorrow."

Calvin looked at them, and Harry said, "Yeah, Calvin, go ahead. Please take a ride and enjoy the horse."

That night, Calvin's mind was in a spin. A good spin, though. He took out the horse and rode her around the entire Village. "I want to ask her," he said to Shuga. "I'm going to ask her," he told the horse as he rode swiftly down the narrow trail. "But the question is, will she say yes?"

The horse did not answer him.

Up ahead in the distance, he could see a clearing. He knew there was a small hill up there with a big jump.[16] "If we make the jump, Suga… she'll say yes! Now, get ready! I see it! Are you ready? Jump!" he yelled as they leapt into midair and back down into a perfect landing.

The next day when he arrived back at Crystalina's house, he went in to talk to her parents before seeing her. "Mr. and Mrs. Devine," he announced anxiously. "I want to ask your daughter if she will marry me, and I want to ask you if I can have your blessing?" He paused, watching their faces.

"No kidding," said Rose, smiling. "I'd like to know what took you so long. Right, Harry? Aren't you happy to hear that, Harry?"

"De-light-ed!" exclaimed Harry, and he immediately offered Calvin a lollipop and his blessing.

---

[16] Chicago. "Question 67 & 68"

Calvin relaxed a bit and smiled. "Thank you, but let's hope she says yes!" he told them, and went upstairs to find her.

Later that evening, they went out on the front porch and sat on the swing. "Oh, it feels so good to be outside again," she told him. "And it's such a beautiful starry night with such a lovely moon."

"Crystalina," Calvin began, then he got up and started to pace.

She got up too, and followed him. "What is it, Calvin?" she asked, becoming concerned. He walked down the four front steps and turned back to look up at her. She peered down at him from the top step. "What is it?" she asked again.

He looked up at her from the bottom step and she was looking at him right in the eyes. Then he held out both his arms toward her as he spoke. "I love you and I want you to marry me, Crystalina. There will never be anyone else for me! Please, say you feel the same way. Say you'll marry me?"

He saw with his own eyes the look of pure elation on her face as she jumped right into his arms, and as he caught her, he twirled her around and he held her close.

After a few moments, he said, "Well…? Does that mean *yes*?"

"Yes, yes, and *yes*," she told him.

They sat on the swing for a long time, talking and making plans. Before he left, he began to wonder a little, and said, "Nothing will change your mind, will it?"

She smiled and said, "No. Nothing will change it!"

He smiled, but then added, "You won't get sick of me hanging around you all the time, will you?"

"No, never," she said, and then repeated with a whisper into his ear, "Never, my love."

Later, after he had gone home, she sat there thinking about everything that had happened over the last couple months.[17] A song kept playing in her head and she started singing it. Then, without her even realizing it, most of the neighbors threw open their windows and joined in the chorus, and the next thing she knew, all of them were singing and dancing in the jeweled street.

"The gig is set and practically written in stone!" cried Dapper to his father after hearing word of Calvin and Crystalina.

"I knew it—I told you that you had to go up that darn mountain to find her," yelled Biffer.

"Well, it's too late for that now! She even gave me back the ring! Listen, Pop, you gotta fix this thing for me!" Dapper rattled.

Biffer nodded his head, "Yeah, I know, son. I'll think of something. Go on up to bed and I'll talk to Aunt Jayja in the morning."

The next morning, Aunt Jayja was preparing the dog food when Biffer came in to speak to her. In a matter of

[17] 5th Dimension. "Never My Love"

ten minutes, everyone in the house was yelling, crying and screaming. "Well, none of you are going to attend that darn wedding!" Biffer ordered.

Then, all at once, the triplets began crying and screaming in unison. "We are, too!" stormed Birdy with her arms folded across her chest.

"Crystalina's our friend!" declared Swobbie, and then crying, she said, "and I wanna wear my new dress!"

"Dapper's a big, fat coward!" yelled Beaky.

Dapper stormed up to her. "Hey! Who you callin' a coward! You long beaked honker, you!" hollered Dapper to Beaky.

"Now, you three girls listen to me! You're not going, and that's that! Don't you have any loyalty to your brother?" He didn't want to hear any more of their crying so he said, "Get upstairs, all of you!"

When they finally left the room, Biffer said to Jayja, "They're going to pay for this one. Nobody dumps my son!"

"Oh, come on, Biff! Knock it off, will ya!" said Jayja. "Here—have some breakfast," she said, sliding the plate of dog food over to him. She watched him as he was devouring the dog food and making threats in between bites. "Ya know, she was never right for Dapper, anyway." Aunt Jayja announced. "Why, I'm surprised he never took up with that—what's her name over there, ah—Karess. Yes, that's her name. Why, she's very glamorous and a smart business woman too."

"All I know is that I've tried to give these kids everything, and I tell them one little thing and all I hear is defiance. I'm going to work, where at least the people there listen to what I have to say!" Biffer announced, then, turning back, he said, "Good breakfast, Jayja!"

Later, when Aunt Jayja knocked on Dapper's bedroom door, she went in to find him combing his hair. "Where are you heading, all spiffed up like that?" Aunt Jayja asked suspiciously.

"Well, Auntie, I heard what you said about Karess, and after thinking it over, I think you may have a good idea there. So, I thought I'd just take a little swing by her place and see what's poppin'."

Aunt Jayja chuckled, "Now you're talkin', or poppin'," she agreed.

Everyone in the Village received an invitation to the wedding. It was to be held at dawn, when the sun was rising over the mountain. Hedda was thrilled for Calvin and agreed to be his best man. "Hey, I wouldn't miss it, man!" Then he even offered to make the biggest and best wedding cake for them.

Crystalina took Stacey to Bully's with her and told her she wanted a different wedding dress. "Something white, but very soft and billowy."

"I think I have just the right dress." Bully announced and told Crystalina to try it on for them.

When she came out of the dressing room, Bully gasped, and with tears in her eyes, she added the veil. “Yes, there is no question,” said Bully, “that’s the one.”

Stacey nodded, “Wow, it’s beautiful on you, really beautiful. You look like an angel.”

Crystalina agreed, “It’s so soft and long. It’s absolutely perfect, exactly what I hoped it would be.”

“What about your bridesmaids?” asked Bully?

“Well, Stacey is here now, and Kell and Suey will be in to see you soon.”

“Great!” Bully said. “And, Crystalina, I’m very happy for you. I can see that you’re really in love this time!”

The weeks flew by and, finally, the wedding was near. The day before, in the heart of the Village, people were going around tying thick, white ribbons, and in the center of the ribbon, they displayed big bouquets of colored roses every few feet.

Carlton’s was busy making preparations for the feast. The finest of foods were being cooked and no detail would be spared. The meal was to be made with the most succulent meats, served with luxurious sauces and stuffing of wild rice, with glorious salads with mixed greens and champagne dressings. First though, would come the petite appetizers, and they were to be elegantly placed around huge fountains that would flow with pink, bubbling champagne. Carlton with the help of his wife, Feather, brought out the best china and crystal, then they personally inspected every glass, dish and piece of silverware to make sure it sparkled.

Round tables were set outside, decorated with white cloths and ribbons, and each had a bouquet of the multicolored roses. Placed in the center of each bouquet was a candle that was to be lit at dawn. The table for the bride and groom was long and had enough room to seat the whole wedding party. A small table was wheeled out and covered with a long, pink table cloth that would hold the huge, five-foot-high wedding cake that Hedda had made. The band had set up a special stage to perform on, and Destiny was invited to sing. They would dance right on the jeweled streets of Morningstar.

Many volunteers helped to set up chairs at the foot of the Mountain, where the actual ceremony would be held. A long, narrow red carpet was rolled out and would be the aisle the bride would walk down, and on each side of it, there were chairs as well as huge bouquets of flowers in between. A lovely arch was decorated with white roses and white gardenias and was placed at the end of the red carpet, and that was to be where Preacher Quentin would perform his nuptials. It was a beautiful display, and it held a heavenly scent. All was prepared for the wedding to begin at daybreak.

Meanwhile, Karess had decided she was definitely not going to the wedding. She was furious about losing Calvin for good, and furious at that witch for giving her a potion that didn't even work. As she sat at her desk slamming things around, Dapper walked in again. He'd been hanging around a lot. He strode up to her, smiling, and this time she took a good, long, hard look at this handsome young thing walking up to her.

"Hi," he said confidently as he stroked his slick hair back with his hand. "I was wondering what you were doing tomorrow?"

Karess looked up at him, surprised, her eyes inspecting him. *He is very attractive*, she thought. *He's no Calvin, but his daddy is rich enough to maybe make up for that. Why didn't I noticed him before?* she wondered. Suddenly, she was in a good mood.

"What'd ya have in mind?" she purred.

Dawn had not yet broken, and Calvin stood at the foot of the mountain with the preacher and Hedda, his best man. Most of the people in the Village had come to witness the union of their love.

The flocks of little, white lovebirds were perched on branches that were hidden in the trees. Even they were rejoicing over the wedding day, and the people could hear their sweet song floating through the air as they sang.

Calvin whispered from the depths of his soul a thank you to God above, who had brought him to this miraculous day. It was more than he had ever dreamed possible, and he never knew that such love and happiness could exist.

The guests all waited expectantly and were seated now on both sides in the predawn morning. They listened as the lovebirds sang on, enchanting them.

Wedding music began to play quietly as the bridesmaids flowed down the aisle, and following them was a little flower girl, dropping white rose pedals. Aside of her was a small ring bearer who carried the rings on a silken pillow. When the bridesmaids were at the altar, they turned to face the guests. Then two tall men appeared at the end of the aisle, each one holding a trumpet.

The preacher raised his arms in the air and announced, "Everyone, please rise."

The two men at the end of the aisle blew their trumpets as the people stood. Then the bride appeared, veiled and draped in white. Everyone gasped at the beauty of her, and Calvin's eyes lit up and his heart started to beat faster.

She began to walk down the aisle with her father by her side. He had worn his wooden leg, and under his handsome tuxedo, you would never even know that his leg was made of wood. She looked lovely, all in white, with her dark hair pulled away from her face and cascading down her back under the lovely laced veil. As the bridal music played, she slowly floated down the aisle toward Calvin.

Her father kissed her with tears of pride and joy as he presented her to him. He then went to his seat beside

Rose, who could not hold back her tears of happiness either. Her sister, Leelee, consoled her while Jayja gave her another handkerchief.

As Calvin took her arm and they faced the preacher, he could feel every fiber of his begin tingling inside, and he knew it was his heart overflowing with joy. The preacher spoke, and they took their vows and made promises to keep each other for the rest of their lives. Just when the preacher was to pronounce them husband and wife, the sun rose up over the mountaintop, and then burst forth, forming into a rainbow as it arched over them in the sky. It was at that second that Calvin felt his spirit rise up too, and suddenly join with hers, and he knew they had become one.

"You may kiss the bride," the preacher told him.

Calvin gently lifted the veil and put his hands on each side of her face. She looked into his eyes and he kissed her then, with all the love and tenderness he had felt for her.

The people began to applaud and rose to their feet, and not a dry eye was among them.

Then, the lovebirds flew above them and, forming a heart, they sang, "Hallelujah!" anointing them with peace, happiness, and love forever more.

The wedding day was filled with celebration. Songs and dancing, lovely foods, and the wedding cake was a masterpiece, done all in white with colored roses decorating each layer.

They ate and danced into the night. Then the band played a special song for them, and everyone cleared the way to watch the newlyweds dance together.[18] Everyone who watched them agreed they were so right together, so very blessed.

At the end of the evening, Crystalina threw the bouquet and was glad that Stacey had caught it. Then the new married couple left in the decorated coach that would bring them to set sail at midnight, on a ship for two weeks, alone.

When the newlyweds returned from their glorious honeymoon at sea, they went to Calvin's house, where they had planned to live together. Most of Crystalina's things were already there. Her mother and aunts had brought over all the cards and gifts from the wedding and placed them all on the table for the couple to open when they returned. It felt like Christmas Day to them as they opened the cards and gifts together. One gift, though, had no card, so they opened it. Inside was a big, gray rock, and painted on the stone was writing that read, "Your time will come!" Calvin looked at his wife. She looked at the rock. They looked at each other.

"Who do you think gave us this?" asked Crystalina. Then they both said it at the same time: "Snip!"

"What do you think he will do?" she asked him.

[18] Graham, Larry. "One in a Million You"

Calvin got up and threw the rock in the trash. "Whatever he does is up to him. I have you and, to me, that is all that matters," he told her, smiling. Then he kissed the tip of her nose.

"It's true," she said as she smiled back at him. "We have each other, and I won't let anyone spoil our happiness again."

As the days turned into weeks, Calvin and Crystalina could not have been happier. Crystalina set about decorating their little house, and Calvin helped her by making her many pieces of furniture that she loved.

She practiced her cooking and tried out new recipes on him, and he told her he loved everything she made for him. The only thing she felt she couldn't get right was the laundry. She'd wash the clothes, hang them on the line to dry, and then stand back, look at it, and then she'd take it all down again and rewash it. No matter what she did, she could not seem to get the clothes *as white as milk*, like her mother had.

Calvin made it a point to write to Mrs. Tag to tell her about his marriage. He also sent a note to his stepmother. As usual, Mrs. Tag had written right back, and she was of course very happy for him. And, as usual, he hadn't heard a word from his stepmother.

"Someday, you'll hear from her," Crystalina told him.

"Oh, yeah? How do you know that?" he asked.

"Who could forget you?" she said.

Calvin's job at the wheel factory was becoming unbearable. Ever since Dapper became engaged to marry Karess, he had begun to work with Calvin. Apparently, it was decided that if a man was mature enough to marry, he had better have a job. Dapper was made floor supervisor. That meant that he would be Calvin's boss. Not only did Dapper not know what he was doing, he hardly ever did anything, except order Calvin around. He'd order Calvin to pack up some of the wheels. After hours of work and sweat, Calvin would complete the job, and then Dapper would tell him it was all wrong. He announced that the wheels were to have been packed in the blue boxes, not the white boxes, and then they were to be stacked in the shipping room. Then he told Calvin that he didn't listen and that he had better stay late and fix it and not to dare think he would be paid for overtime to fix his own mistakes. Then, Dapper would fold up his newspaper, sign out, and go home, while Calvin would stay late and redo the whole job.

In the morning, Dapper started pulling a new trick. Calvin would always arrive right on time, and sometimes ten or fifteen minutes early. He would sign in, but he noticed that, recently, Dapper had been erasing his time card and writing in a time that made him ten or fifteen minutes late.

One night, when Calvin arrived home late, Crystalina asked if everything was going all right with work. He told her everything was fine, that he just had some extra work to do. He decided that Dapper would stop his little game sooner or later, and, for now, he did not want to upset his new wife, so he kept his work problems to himself.

He couldn't help but notice that she was grinning from ear to ear and seemed excited about something. He laughed, "What is it?'

"What's what?" she answered chuckling and smiling.

He walked over to her and stared at her while she was stirring something on the stove. As he stared at her, smiling, she could not hold back any longer or she would burst from the excitement. She said, "Calvin, we're going to have a baby!"

Calvin was absolutely thrilled, and that evening they went for a long walk and talked and laughed and planned for hours.

As the weeks went on, Calvin was becoming more and more concerned about his job. Instead of getting better, Dapper was getting worse. He began to wish that he could find those diamonds people had talked about for so long, so he could leave Dapper and the job he was growing to despise.

Now that they were expecting a child, Calvin would often go out and work on the cradle he was making for the baby, while Crystalina made curtains and knitted soft baby blankets. They were so excited about the baby, they could hardly wait.

One day, Calvin was called home from work. He ran to the house wondering what could possibly have happened. When he came through the door, he found Rose there with the doctor. Crystalina was in bed, crying. The doctor stopped him before he went to her. He told Calvin that she had lost the baby. "I'm sorry," the doctor told him. "I think it may be due to the accident on the mountain a time ago, some unseen injury. I'm not quite sure yet, but after examining her, I don't think it will be possible for her to have any children."

After that day, their lives changed. It was like a dark cloud had befallen them. Crystalina was so sad all the time. He tried hard to help her, but nothing seemed to change her mood. He even put away the cradle, blankets, clothes, and everything else that kept reminding them of their loss.

He knew she was trying desperately to pull herself out of her grief and act cheerful for his sake, but it just was not working. Finally, though after a long while, she started to go out again. One afternoon she went into the Village, and she ran into Karess, who was dying to show off her huge engagement ring.

As she flashed her ring about, she asked, "Isn't it grand?"

Crystalina nodded as she said, "Oh, its great! Well, I hope you two will be very happy," she added sincerely.

Karess's eyes flashed, "Oh, you bet we'll be happy, honey, and I plan on givin' him plenty of children too! Sorry to hear about your baby. Ain't it just a shame you can't give that handsome husband of yours a child," she said arrogantly before striding off.

Crystalina tried not to get upset, but when she tried to hold in her grief and sorrow, she began to quiver and she just burst into tears. She leaned on something for a moment, and then hurried home as fast as she could, feeling so foolish that she had cried right in the middle of the Village. When she got home she fell to pieces. She just could not bear the pain of losing her baby, and, most of all, to never be able to have a child was too much for her to bear.

As time went on, she actually began to dread waking up in the morning and getting out of bed, only to face the pain of it all again.

On his way home one evening, Calvin thought that he had better tell Crystalina about what was happening at work, and though he did not want to upset her anymore, he knew he had to do something soon. It seemed now that it was never going to change with Dapper, they would have to talk about it sooner or later. But when he walked in the door, he changed his mind when he saw that she had been crying. They sat together, and she told him exactly what had happened the afternoon she went into the Village. After hearing Karess remind her of the baby they lost, the babies they would never have, she could not bear it. He held her close and wished so badly that he could make it better for her.

After hours of talk, they finally fell asleep, and that night he had a dream he was standing in a blue mist and someone was speaking to him; "Calvin," the voice said, "God has heard the cries of your wife and the desire of your heart. You will have a child. He will give you a son. You will call him Matteus. And as a sign of your faith, you will call your wife 'Mother,' and she will call you, 'Father.' You will continue to do this until what I have told you this night comes true. God will hear you, and he will give you your child, which will be his gift to you."

When Calvin woke in the morning, he remembered the dream as vividly and as he had done before, he wrote it down in his journal. When Crystalina woke, he told her everything that was said to him in the dream. Then he told her how the angel had come to him in a dream before saying God would protect him. And then right afterward, he had been saved from the fall in the balloon. Then he told her about the quiet voice he had heard that had told him that she was *the one*, when he had seen her that very first time at the waterfall.

"I don't know, Calvin. How we can hang onto hope when I already lost one child, and I've been told by the doctor—"

Calvin did not let her finish what she was saying. He put his hands on her two arms and looked into her eyes. "It's true, Crystalina, what the angel said to me, and you've got to be with me on this. You've got to believe! It's the only way!" he said, pleading with her.

"You really believe that, don't you?" she asked in surprise.

"Yes, I do." he answered. "And there is one more thing the voice said to me."

"What is it?" she asked.

"Well, as a sign of our faith, I am supposed to call you Mother Crystalina, and you're supposed to call me Father Calvin." They both burst out laughing. "Say 'okay,' Mama," he said, smiling.

She looked at him, right into his eyes to be sure he actually meant what he was saying. "Okay, Papa," she answered, giggling.

He hugged her close, "You'll see," he told her. "I promise you, we will have our son!"

So, they went through the days saying *mother* this and *father* that, just as he'd been told to in the dream. At first, they laughed each time they said it, but soon they both fully believed that they would have their child, as promised.

It was just a little over one year later, and Calvin and Crystalina had their miracle baby. It was a boy and they named him Matteus, which meant "gift of God." He was perfect, healthy and strong, and they literally jumped for joy!

12
The Beast

The thick forest seemed dark and menacing. The days were endless, and the nights were cold, with damp echoes of the past always bouncing off the hard cave walls.

Moona could hardly ever bring herself to venture outside the dark, lonely cave she had hidden herself in for so long. She was lost, lost in the past and lost in the voices in her mind that reminded her unceasingly of her regret and ultimate despair.

When she thought back to what Evana had said to her so long ago, she almost wished she had never married Kanodia at all. "Maybe Evana was right all along," she'd tell herself. "I was never good enough for him! Look at me now, a complete failure." Then she'd look around her dark, sparse cave and remember the beautiful place she had shared with Kanodia. She thought of the enchanting waterfall and even recalled the sound of it as it poured into the deep, blue quarry. She missed the warm hearth the others had made for them. They would set it ablaze on cold nights and watch the jewels beset within the stones begin to dazzle, flashing like prisms of colored light around the flames. They'd sit together watching it for hours.

She remembered it all far too well. The memories that played in her mind over and over again, day in and day out, sent her reeling into the depths of despair. She often thought that maybe it would have been better if she had never known happiness at all.

Moona was only sure of one thing now, and that was that she could never return to the pack. She could never face them again. It was too painful to look at them or even see them and know that they were thinking what a failure she was. It was enough just to have to face it herself! And how could she ever burden Kanodia with the fact that she could never give him the child he deserved to have, that she knew he wanted? "No," she told herself out loud. "I will never return."

Many times over the years, Manny had sent the wolves out to frantically search for Kanodia, but they never found him. When the jeweled, majestic scepter the pack had given him had suddenly disappeared shortly after he left them, Manny was certain that it was a sign that Kanodia was near. But still, after forming an all-out search, looking everywhere they could think of, they never found a trace of him again.

It was too difficult for Manny to let any of the wolves go off to find Kanodia now. The hyenas had grown so large in number; they had become a huge threat to the wolves and he could not afford to let even one wolf leave his post. He was in charge of all of them now, and it was all up to him to keep the pack, the land, their babies, and their food protected.

Manny and Evana had five cubs now, and though his wife cared for them and tended to them, Manny was far more protective. He would give them warning each day that they were not to dare wander from the camp, where he had wolves posted night and day to guard them from the hyenas, but even more from their evil leader, Beast.

He had to listen to them daily, to all their complaints, telling him they were hungry because he would not allow them to venture far enough from their camp to find food. But Manny was absolutely sure of one thing, and that was as hungry as the wolves might be, the hyenas were starved and would sink to any level for a good meal. They would even steal one of their babies to eat.

Manny wished even more than the others that Kanodia would return. Nothing had been the same since he left the pack. Once, Manny thought he would have loved being their leader. But now that he was, the burden was far too much to handle. The very lives of all of them were his complete responsibility and his duty that weighed heavily on his mind and heart each and every day.

Beast slithered between the hyenas, swinging his long neck from left to right. He even looked different from the rest of them. He was pure black and much longer, much smarter, and he knew it. He always knew just when to expose his massive claws, but he restrained his dripping saliva, unlike the other unsophisticated ones.

One of his other secret weapons were his fangs. They were huge and pointy and as sharp as a sword.

When Beast got angry, his eyes turned a crimson red; the color of blood.

Even with all this, it wasn't what made him their leader and kept them under his complete control. It was the fact that there were no lengths he would not go to. Nothing was too evil, or low, or mean, or rotten for him to do to them, and none of them could ever feel safe, for he would betray them on a whim.

Sometimes he would befriend one or two of them. His best choice was always a paired couple. He'd begin acting as if they were his favorite, his only friends. He'd offer them the first selection of meat, and even allow them to eat with him. He'd often take them aside and tell them little secrets. He would act concerned for them and allow them to nap. He would send the hyenas out and let the couple remain with him while the others were on the hunt for their food.

Then, when he would find out that the couple were expecting a baby, he would treat them even better until the child was born. Then, of course, he would expect them to simply give him their child to do with whatever he wished.

When the parents would adamantly refuse, Beast would very calmly, very quietly, order them all out to the river where the huge waterfall flowed. He would announce to all of them that it was to be the place they would hold an important meeting. When everyone arrived, Beast would again give the new parents their chance to change their mind and give him their baby. When they refused, Beast would take the baby, as quickly as you could blink, into his fanged mouth and fling the poor, tiny thing right over the waterfall.

When the parents would attack, as Beast knew they would, he was prepared. He would order his loyal guards to *seize them,* and the guards would throw the parents over the huge, crushing falls too, never to be seen or heard from again.

Beast would laugh as he watched them. Then he'd turn back to the pack of horrified hyenas and shout, "Let that be a lesson to you all!" Then he'd show his fangs again, while his eyes began to turn blood red, and let out another shout, "Any of you who even *thinks* about defying me will be *destroyed*!" He roared as he raised his head up toward the sky. "And especially after I've shown *so much hospitality*! You'll be tossed away like a bird bone, sucked dry of the last bit of flesh, *and I'll love every minute of it,*" he roared again. Then, to prove his determination, out of nowhere, he showed them a bone. He put the bone in his mouth, in between his sharp fangs, as if he were really sucking dry their last bit of flesh. Then, laughing, he stood up on his hind legs, and the other hyenas began to whimper and whine as they started to slowly inch back, fearing he would lunge for one of them. They dared not move too fast, but saw him while he flashed his long claws, each claw looking like a razor-sharp dagger, while he peered at the small, frail bone, squinting his blood-red eyes. And then he snapped it in two and tossed it into the raging waterfall, then he threw back his head and opened his mouth wide, fangs and all, roaring, "*I am the ruler here; the one and only king of the forest*," and let out what sounded something between an evil, sinister laugh and a roar that boomed throughout the whole forest.

The other hyenas squealed for their lives and ran off frantically in every direction.

A few days had passed and Beast sat at his table drumming his claws on the wood. This was not a good sign, his loyal guards knew, and tried to stay out of his way as they trembled to hear what their ruler was upset about today.

"This will not do," Beast exclaimed, and then repeated as he practically spit the words at them, "This *will not do* at all!" He peered back at them with disgust. "Well, call a meeting! Make it quick, you useless little worms! *Look at you*, sitting there in the corner, trembling like little mice. Call everyone together, and hurry, before I cut off your tails and roast them before your very cowardly eyes!"

When all were gathered to him, Beast gave them their final instruction and warning. "I have given you worms as many chances as I plan to give you. Let me make myself clear, this will be the *very last chance you will get!*" He swanned his long neck forward from his podium. "We outnumber these wolves now two to one, and that is the way I intend to keep it!

Now, I get what I want—or else! And this is the last time you will hear this from me, because I *will not wait* any longer. *Find Kanodia* and *destroy* him, once and for *all time*! Leave no stone unturned! And as proof, you will bring me back his scepter!" He rose up on his hind feet, adding, "It should have been *mine* all along, if you rodents had done your job!" Beast calmed himself down. "Now, ten of you will go out again, and you will destroy him and bring your master back the *scepter*!" He smiled at the thought of it. "Now, whoever does this will be rewarded greatly, and you all know that I keep my promises! Go now, quickly! And remember, *I'll be waiting!*"

Days turned to weeks, and Beast was growing more and more impatient as he waited with the others for the news. The longer he waited, the angrier and meaner he became. He would take a few of the hyenas and hang them upside down on ropes, for all the others to view for days, as their tongues hanged out of their mouths, and until they were so dry, so weak, they could not even beg for a drop of water. Then Beast would announce to all, "They better get him, or else they're gonna pay!"

Finally, there was news that they were on their way back. When the anxious hyenas appeared before their master, they were delighted to tell him the news: Kanodia was finally dead! They stood watching as Beast began to smile from ear to ear.

"And…?" asked Beast. They all held their breath while they brought forward the proof their leader had required. They set the royal scepter before their king.

Word spread throughout the forest that the hyenas had destroyed Kanodia, and that they had the scepter to prove it. Finally, Manny had no choice but to hold an important meeting with all of the wolves. When he made the announcement, that Kanodia was dead, word even somehow got back to Moona. The whole pack had gone into utter mourning and agreed to raise a memorial for their cherished, most famous leader, so that he would never be forgotten.

Meanwhile, Seneca, who had only been very small when Kanodia had left the pack, remembered how he had saved him from going down the frigid river rapids. He remembered how the strong wolf had raced beside the raging river, and then Kanodia just dove right in to pull him out of the waters that were sweeping him away, and he returned him to his parents safely.

Seneca attended all the memorials for Kanodia, and he noticed Moona hidden behind the trees, listening to all of it. Every wolf attended, and they were all in deep grief. Seneca saw Moona's parents looking old and sad too, and they cried together, and he knew they felt like they had not only lost Kanodia, but their daughter too. He had heard that they had made so many attempts to lure Moona back into the pack, but it was hopeless, they knew. She was never coming back either.

Many wolves got up to speak about Kanodia's bravery, recalling something heroic he had done for them that had helped them in their lives. There were countless stories, and everyone knew he was a true hero, *their hero*. And now he was gone. There would be no more wishing, hoping, and expecting him to come back to them anymore.

When it was over, Seneca decided to follow Moona. As he hid outside her cave, he could hear her desperate sobbing. Then he heard her as she cried, "What have I done? What have I done? It's all my fault! I never thought he would stay away this long! I wanted him to take another wife, to have the children he deserved. Now it's over and he's gone forever! Oh why? Why? Why?" She cried on and on as if nothing in the world could ever console her broken heart again.

Seneca felt very sorry for her. He slept outside her cave, wondering, as he fell asleep, what he could do to help her. While he slept, he dreamed of Kanodia, and when he woke in the morning, he began thinking about it.

"Kanodia, dead? I don't know, he seemed so alive in the dream!" he said out loud to himself. He decided to investigate it on his own. And with that, the brave young wolf left the pack and journeyed out alone into the forbidden forest to find out the truth.

He had started out so sure of himself, but soon learned that if he didn't keep himself well hidden, he would sooner or later be found and eaten.

Weeks of searching left the young wolf weak, hungry, tired, and, worst of all, lost. Finally, with his last bit of strength, he climbed the tallest hill he could see in the forest. Once at the top, he didn't care anymore. He could not stay quiet or hidden any longer; he just had to find him. So he began to shout at the top of his voice, "Kanodia! Kanodia! Kanodia!" He called over and over again for hours, and then called him some more. Finally, his voice began to get hoarse, and he simply could not call out anymore. It was dark outside, except for the full moon, and out of complete and utter exhaustion, he lay down, and, in a matter of moments, fell asleep.

The next morning, the little wolf opened his eyes, feeling alarmed when he heard some footsteps coming toward him.

He was shocked when, standing before him, was Kanodia, as alive as could be! The young, brave Seneca hoped he wasn't dreaming again, and he just sat there staring at him. Then he heard Kanodia say,

"You called?"

13
Gone in the Night

Karess and Dapper were married. When they returned from their honeymoon, Calvin was abruptly informed that he was being fired from his job for constantly being late. Even worse, he was told that he had one week to move out of the house that Biffer Snip was renting him. Dapper and Karess would be living there while their elaborate new home was being built to their ideal specifications.

Calvin knew that there was no sense in trying to argue by telling his boss he had never been late even once, or that it was totally unfair to ask him to move his family in less than one week. He already knew, and had known for quite a while, that Biffer Snip and Dapper had it out for him because of his marriage to Crystalina and that now they would carry out their evil deeds.

Now what am I going to do, Calvin thought as he walked home. *How will I tell Crystalina?* Calvin wondered angrily. He hated most that it was harming his family to have to uproot them like this, and all of that to go where? He didn't know.

He broke the news to his wife the following morning, figuring there was no sense in ruining her whole evening. She immediately suggested moving to her parents' home, but he told her he just needed a little time to think things over.

Crystalina asked him, "Calvin, what is there to think over? We have nowhere else to go!"

Calvin took a deep breath and sighed. "I don't think that is the right thing to do," he told her.

She gave him a look of bewilderment, and he went out for a walk. He strode through the meadows and back to the gazebo, where he had gone so many times to listen to the waters of the quarry and to think. When he sat down at the water's edge, he couldn't help but talk out loud to himself.

"I don't want to live with her parents. I want to be able to care for my own family," he announced. Then he took his carving knife out of his pocket and grabbed a branch and began to carve out something, some piece of wood furniture, though he had nothing in mind yet. He whittled away for what seemed to be a long time, and then lay back while his feet still dangled in the water. He closed his eyes, and looking up he asked, "What's the answer?"

It was night now and the moon was close to full. He pulled himself up and grabbed his knife and the branch that he had begun to carve. As he held the would-be furniture in his hand, he shouted out loud, "That's it! That is the answer!"

He hurried back to the house and went in to tell his wife the plan. He explained to her what his father had done after their home was destroyed. He told her how he had just started to build his own house. He held up the branch explaining also that that was how their furniture business had started.

Crystalina was still bewildered. “Well, does that mean you’re going to start a furniture business?”

Calvin shook his head. “No, it means I’m going to build us our own house.”

“How?” she asked. “Biffer owns all the land in Morningstar, and the land he has for sale is priced so high, we could never afford it!”

Calvin nodded his head, “I know, I know. That is why I am going into the forest to build our home.” He stood, looking at her, watching her surprised expression, and then he went on. “You and the baby will stay with your parents, and I will go into the forest and find us the perfect spot. When the house is ready, I will come back for you.” She stared at him and said nothing. “After we move, I can make furniture and bring it into the Village to sell. Then we’ll get the supplies we need from the Village and bring them back with us. I can catch fish for us, and we can load up on fruits and berries from the Village every week.” Calvin took a drink of his water, “We’ll visit, honey, every week, and please don’t look at me like that. I can’t stand to see you looking so sad.”

There was silence between them for a long moment. Finally, Crystalina spoke, “I’m not sad,” she said. “Actually, it sounds perfect. Just like a true adventure, like we’ll really be out there, on our own.”

Calvin went over and hugged her, holding her tight.

They packed up their belongings, and Crystalina couldn't help shedding a few tears over leaving their first home together. After all, it was where they had started, and she had so many good memories of long nights with her husband, and it had been the house where their beautiful baby was born. It was hard for both of them to leave all of it behind them, but they knew that it was time to go.

Once he had gotten Crystalina and the baby settled at her parent's home, he packed a sleeping bag and a few tools. Then, with hardly anything but his wits, he set off to find himself the perfect place to build his family a home of their own.

They said a tearful goodbye to each other, but he promised he would return as soon as he could for them. Crystalina insisted he take the horse, and Calvin was glad to have the company. "Be careful," she told him through her tears, as she waved goodbye to him. He smiled back at them and wondered how long it would be until he could be with them again.

Calvin wandered through the forest, looking for just the right spot to build. He tied small pieces of material to branches along the way, so that he could find his way back to the Village. Finally, he had found a clear spot in the midst of all the huge trees, which was near a slow-moving fresh water stream.

"This is the place," he declared. He made a stake and drove it forcefully into the ground, right in the center of the land. Then he tied a piece of thin, red-colored material around the stake, and said out loud to himself, "This is where we will build our home and this is where we will live!"

He got to work the very next morning. He began by chopping down some trees and carefully measuring out logs that were all the same in size. He chopped wood, cut, pounded, measured, and built from sun up to sun down. It didn't matter if it was sunny, or rainy, or windy; he went on building. At night, he slept under the stars in his sleeping bag, and fell asleep listening to the strange noises and howls of the forest. "I better get used to it," he told the horse, who looked down at him, and Calvin actually thought for one small moment that the horse whispered something to him, like *better you than me.*

But Calvin knew that was impossible, and told himself that animals don't talk and that it must have been a sound in the forest.

Crystalina had packed him every piece of food and berry and fruit that she could fit into a bag, knowing that once he left the walled Village of Morningstar, everything was different. Food was not everywhere, and the weather could be unpredictable, she had heard, and she was so worried he would run out of food or be cold.

Calvin worried that she would hate finding out how hard it could be to even find an edible berry, as he dug through the bag, looking for a banana or something to give him energy for the morning work.

Later that day, as he was chopping away, he thought he was hearing things again when he heard someone call out his name. He began to walk toward the sound.

He heard something, "Who's there? Who are you?" he called.

Then he heard someone coming. "It's us!" they exclaimed, and there stood Hedda and Carlton.

Calvin smiled and stared at them.

"Hey, we heard what Snip pulled on ya, and well, we decided, hey, the guy might be hungry!" Hedda told him as he began to set out a blanket and unfold the most delectable, delicious items Calvin thought he had ever laid eyes on. He was quick to join in for the feast.

"We thought we would stay a few days and help you pull this deal together," Carlton told him. Calvin was speechless; he had never expected that they would do this for him, but he was so happy to see them.

"How in the world did you guys even find me?" he asked.

"We just followed the red ribbons on the branches!" answered Hedda, smiling.

"Yeah, well, we're workin' it for ya, Cal," Carlton told him.

"Hey, you don't have to tell us now," Hedda said. "But we are really dying to know, do you have plans to go searching for the diamond mines?"

"You know, I've been thinking about it a lot, to be honest, I don't know where to begin to search. We definitely could use the finances if we ever want to be able to live in Morningstar again. Snip will never let us rent another place from him for sure, and if we want to buy our own home it seems so pricey…."

Hedda nodded. "I get it man, you need it, but it's not worth it man. It can be really dangerous out here in the forest. I don't want to be worrying about you."

"I know, I know," Calvin agreed. "I have a wife and son so I'm not going to do anything without thinking it through carefully. No worries! It's going to be great; it's going to all work out."

"Sounds cool man, so now that we got that out of the way, and our stomachs are full, let's gets to work!" Hedda said.

And they did.[19] They all began to work together, and they even developed a rhythm. Calvin would climb, cut and throw, while the two men would nail, pound and catch. Then Calvin would saw and sand, while they would chop and chisel. Somehow it was working, as they talked about how hard it was becoming to live in Morningstar, when Snip owned all the land and practically all the houses. They still managed to joke and laugh as they worked. After a few days of nonstop hard work, it was really beginning to look like a little house.

Calvin hated to see Carlton and Hedda go, but they had to get back.

---

[19] Chicago. "Dialog"

"I'll never forget what you guys did for me," Calvin told them sincerely.

"Ah, forget about it!" they both said, smiling. "We'll tell Crystalina that the house is almost ready."

"Yes, tell her I miss her and I'll be back soon!" Calvin said, then added, "Listen, you guys, I'm going to miss—"

Hedda stopped him, gesturing with his hand, "Hey, now that we know where you live, you'll see us all the time. You'll never get rid of us!"

As usual, Hedda got them all laughing.

"Keep up the good work," they told him.

"Hey, thanks, friends!" Calvin said, and he meant it, as he watched them walk into the forest.

After who knew how long it was, the house was finally ready, and Calvin stood back and looked at it. Satisfied that it was a start for them, he could not get back to his wife and baby fast enough.

As Calvin approached the Village, he rode toward her house, and he could see her from a distance and she saw him too. He watched as she handed the baby to her mother and began to run down the street toward him. He quickly got off the horse and ran to her. They hugged each other tightly, so thankful to be together again.

Calvin then went in to see his son, who was looking healthy and happy. Harry and Rose gave him a big welcome too, and they all sat down to dinner together.

The next day, they began to pack up a wagon with all their belongings. Crystalina told him she was dying to see their home. They jammed as much of their stuff into the wagon as they could and, again, packed up bushels of fruits and berries. It wasn't long after that that they said their goodbyes, and Rose and Harry watched them tearfully as they set off for their new life in their little home out in the forest. After walking for a long time into the woods, they finally arrived at the little house, and Calvin actually carried her over the threshold again. She told him it was lovely, and she immediately began to set up each little room. There was a kitchen, and a parlor with a big hearthstone fireplace, as well as two small bedrooms. It had so much charm and smelled of clean, fresh wood.

As the days went by, Calvin made more furnishings for their home, while Crystalina cared for the baby, washed their clothes in the stream, and often fought bugs with her broom when they tried to come into the house. Then at night, he would run down to the stream and catch some fish for them to eat.

They were happy and content, all together in their own little home, and that was what mattered most of all to them. Everything was peaceful, and they were happy. Sometimes Calvin mentioned looking for the diamond mines, but Crystalina would immediately get upset, fearing something terrible might happen to him, as she had heard it told several times. Calvin decided to put that mission on hold for a while.

In the middle of the night, Crystalina often woke to check on the baby. But one night, Calvin woke to the sounds of screaming.

“What is it?” he called as he ran to her.

“The baby!” she cried, pointing to the empty cradle. “He’s gone!”

Calvin’s eyes darted around the room, and then he said frantically, “Quick, check under the bed. Check everywhere while I check outside!”

He grabbed a long stick he had made into a torch and lit it in the low flame of the hearth. He ran outside looking around in desperation. It was dark. It was the middle of the night, and he was trying to see something, anything, while listening for the baby’s sounds, a cry, something!

Then he saw them, and a fear rose up in him. It was an overwhelming fear, and he thought that fear itself would devour him. There, in the damp, raw dirt, were the unmistakable, deep impressions of wolf tracks.

Just at that moment, Crystalina burst out of the door, shouting that the baby was nowhere to be found. Then she saw Calvin looking at the tracks in the wet dirt. She saw the fear that was in his eyes when he looked at her, and she began to scream, “No! No! No!” She backed up as she cried, almost hysterical, then, when her back hit the house, she slid down against it, crying uncontrollably as she spoke, “My baby! Please, God, no. Not my little baby!”

Calvin went to her, but there was no time for any words of comfort. He was shaking when he said, “Crystalina, I’ll find him. Stay in the house! Barricade the doors and the windows and pray. Pray, pray!” It was all he could say. He had to leave immediately to find their baby. Their sweet, beautiful, tiny baby.

"Oh, God," Calvin whispered, "lead me to him, please! Save him. Protect him, please!" And then he ran, following the tracks the wolf had left in the dirt.

He followed the trail for a long time. Sometimes he had to make a guess, because the dirt was too hard, or the leaves were piled up along the path. Sometimes grass covered over any tracks. Soon, though, he was able to pick up the trail again, once by spotting a broken branch that had some fur on it.

He was so deep within the huge forest now, he wondered for a moment how he would ever find his way back again. He had to stop to make more torchlight. When he began to follow the trail again, he thought he heard something following him. At first, he hoped it was his imagination, but he knew, deep down, it was not. He stopped for a moment; it had been so hard just to keep calm and now, this. He listened intently and heard an eerie sound, like a laugh, but he knew that sound and it wasn't human, and the evil noise was coming from over his head. He looked up, and hidden in the trees, he saw a long, big, black animal leering at him with blood in his eyes.

"Where's my son?" Calvin yelled. All he heard was the evil laugh again, and saw the jet black animal jump to what seemed to be the top of another tree. He could not see him anymore. "Where is he?" he demanded again.

No answer. He could waste no more time, and began to follow the wolf tracks again. He held the lit torch low so he could see the tracks. Then, the worst thing happened; he felt a raindrop.[20] "No—" he thought. "Not rain. It will wash away all the tracks!" But it was no use, the wind picked up, and the rain fell so hard, it put out the torch.

"No!" screamed Calvin.

He heard the evil laugh again, this time louder, and it bellowed through the forest within the sound of the clattering rain. Then it spoke. It was a low, sadistic, moaning voice that said, "You'll never find him now! Hee, hee, ha, ha!"

Calvin was devastated as he looked up toward the treetops, trying to see where the evil thing was. Then he saw the black sky part, and a bolt of lightning lit the sky, cutting through it like a sharp, jagged spear as it hit the tail of the black hyena, scorching it right off.

He heard it yelp and screech and roar as it jumped out of the trees and ran off in a tailless scurry. Calvin stood there in the dark, soaked from head to toe, all the wolf tracks, now washed away. He sat down against a tree and put his head in his hands.

"Please, God, help me. What can I do now? My baby! Please, keep him safe somehow," he pleaded helplessly.

When he looked up, he was surrounded by at least ten hyenas that were staring at him, licking their chops, their eyes glowing in the dark, wet depths of the night.

[20] Electric Light Orchestra. "Standin' in the Rain"

They slowly began to move in closer to him. Calvin stood up, and with nowhere to go, he said, “No, please, I have to find my baby—my son!”

They didn’t care. They licked their dripping jowls and prepared to leap on him. Then they began to sway and snort and growl, as if they were arguing amongst themselves as to who would get the first bite.

Then, the largest hyena of them all leaned back on his hind feet and jumped toward Calvin, but just when the creature was in midair and heading for his throat, a huge wolf appeared out of the darkness and lunged into the hyena’s neck with his huge teeth, and then flung him in one fell swoop. The other hyenas began to back away, but Kanodia was quicker and grabbed another one’s neck and used it to knock them all off their feet, and they tumbled like dominoes, one after another. When they realized he was on the attack again, they all began to scramble to their feet and took off, squealing.

Calvin just sat there, breathless, staring into the golden eyes of the wolf. Kanodia stared back at him. Then the wolf lurched his neck and head to one side as if to say, *follow me.*

Calvin knew nothing else to do, but follow and prayed that, somehow, he would find his baby.

14
The Black Pit

Calvin followed as Kanodia led him toward the caves. He reared his head back toward Calvin, motioning for him to grab the flaming torch that loomed beside the dark cave and follow him inside.

Blinking his eyes to adjust to the firelight, the first thing he saw was a white wolf caring for his infant son.

Calvin's heart raced within him, and he rushed over to his baby, whisking him into his arms and holding him close. "Matteus, my baby. Thank you, God! Thank you!"

He looked into the baby's face, and his son smiled at him, happily cooing.

Calvin looked over at Kanodia, "Why?" he asked with a tear of relief sliding down his cheek.

Kanodia put his head down in shame, but after a moment he made a decision. This decision would break the strictest, most sacred rule in the entire animal kingdom, one that had been kept by all animals since the beginning of time. No one had ever broken it, but Kanodia knew right then and there he had to do it. He actually opened his mouth and he spoke. He said to Calvin, "Please, sit down."

Calvin did sit, but he was in a state of utter shock when he heard the wolf actually speak to him. "Whoa, you talk?" was all he could say.

Kanodia nodded, "It's a rule of the animal kingdom, to never let humans know that we not only understand what they say, but that we can also talk."

Calvin simply nodded his head with his mouth and eyes wide open.

"I took your baby and I am truly sorry for taking him," Kanodia told him. "You see, I did it for my wife." He paused and looked at Moona. "She cannot have children, and it was for that reason that she sent me away so long ago. She then hid away in a dark cave, constantly in despair. This went on for years, and I was so fraught, it had been so long. I know there is no excuse for doing what I did, but I was desperate—" Kanodia told him all the sad details of what had happened to them.

"Yes," Calvin could understand how desperate Moona had felt, but he said, "What did that have to do with taking my son?"

"Don't you see?" Kanodia exclaimed, "Nothing. Nothing could bring her out of that cave!" Kanodia paused, "When the young wolf, Seneca came and found me and explained how desperately in despair Moona was, well, I just didn't think about what that would do to you, or any of the consequences, for that matter! All I could think about was how to save my wife. Unfortunately,

I felt the only thing that could bring her back was to give her a child; someone, something that needed her. I had to give her a reason to live again," Kanodia hung his head. "Then," he said sadly, "After I was done, I heard you in the forest, and your cries of desperation as you searched frantically for your son, and I knew I had done something terribly wrong! Something so against what I believe in, myself. It's no excuse, but if you could find it in you to understand, I acted impulsively. It was wrong, and I am truly, truly, so very sorry." He paused and looked up at Calvin, "Please," he asked, "can you possibly ever forgive me?"

Moona spoke up then, and said to Calvin, "Please, don't blame him. He did it for me. I am the one who needs to be forgiven by both of you. Please!" she begged, "it was my fault entirely!" She turned to Kanodia. "When I saw you alive, well, it was like someone had turned back time! Suddenly I knew it was another chance for us. I realized that your love for me was unconditional. I put us through all this pain for nothing! Please, Kanodia, I hope it's not too much to ask, but please, stay with me now. Will you stay with me forever?"

Kanodia's heart grew at that moment, and he thought it would burst inside of him as it overflowed with joy and relief. He walked over to her and nuzzled against the side of her face and whispered, "Stay with you? Why, it's all I've wanted to hear you say!"

After a few minutes, the wolves realized that Calvin was still sitting there. They both began, again, to feel the remorse for the anguish they had caused him. The wolves whispered something to one another, and they both nodded in agreement. Kanodia spoke first. "We would like to offer you a gift, Calvin. It is probably something that will be very useful to you."

Calvin began to shake his head. "I have to get back to my wife—" he uttered, but before he could say any more, Kanodia interrupted him.

"Please, allow us to do this for you, just to show you how tremendously sorry we really are. It will be quick, and then, I promise, I'll lead you and your baby safely home. Please?" Kanodia pleaded, "Follow me."

In spite of all that had happened, Calvin decided to follow him. What choice did he have anyway? He was very deep in the middle of the forest in the dark, and he would never find his way out alone. He thought that, after all, Kanodia had saved his life. Kanodia even convinced him to let Moona guard the child while he went with Kanodia. He hesitated, but, strangely, he could relate to these two wolves now. Somehow, he trusted them, so he went on to follow the huge wolf.

Kanodia walked him through the forest that led him to another dark cave. He stopped and, before leading him in, Kanodia told him to take the lit torch that was posted outside the cave. Calvin thought it strange that he had been led to another cave, but he took the torch anyway, and went on further, until he felt like they were entering into the very center of the earth as they wound around corners going lower and deeper with each turn. But it was not the center of the earth; it was a place that was actually known as 'the black pit.' When Kanodia stepped through the entryway of the pit, there, huddled together, were countless slathering hyenas. The hyenas gasped with shock at seeing him.

"All of you, out!" Kanodia roared. "I'm back and here to stay for good. As you can see I'm not dead, and I'm taking over now!"

The hyenas trembled, but one of them said, "We... but we thought you were dead!"

"Dead, huh? Just because one of you stole my scepter, huh? Nice try." Kanodia checked out their faces to see who the guilty one might be, "And by the way, where is my scepter? I want it back. Now."

They scurried down to the lowest level of the cave to get their leader, but they returned a few minutes later, alone.

"Well, where is he?"

Just then, Beast appeared before them. "So, Kanodia's alive, and thinks he is going to just take over again, huh?" he said sarcastically.

"I don't think it, Beast. I know it. Why?" Kanodia smirked. "Do you really think you might have any say in what I do?" Kanodia asked. Then he remembered Calvin was with him, and told Beast, "I'm busy now, but you can be sure, I'll catch up with you later. For now, you can keep the scepter. Go, pretend you're the king for a while if you must. Just take your little followers and go. Get out of here now!"

Beast looked back at his scorched tail. Embarrassed and in pain, he knew that he was in no shape to fight this giant wolf, so he called the hyenas. "Let's go, animals!" he ordered.

It took just a few moments for them to clear out, and then Kanodia turned to Calvin. "Follow me; it's just a bit farther." Calvin figured he had gone this far, and, besides, he knew he couldn't find his way back alone now, so he went on with Kanodia.

The wolf led him deeper to the depths of the dark cave, and then Kanodia stopped and said to Calvin, "Now, hold the torch up toward the walls."

Calvin did, and then he saw them. Diamonds! The whole wall was dazzling with them; big, small, and some looked absolutely enormous! Kanodia watched the look of amazement on Calvin's face.

"So, this is where the diamond mines have been all this time?" he whispered.

Kanodia nodded. "And we are giving it to you. All of it, Calvin. It's all yours."

Calvin had to sit down for a moment, so he sat on a large rock, realizing that even the rock he sat on was a huge diamond. "You know, this will make me and my family rich beyond our wildest dreams," he told Kanodia.

Kanodia nodded again. “I hope so,” he said. “It’s the least I could do to try to repay you.”

Calvin smiled, “A lot of good men died trying to find these diamonds, and now I can see why. Thank you!”

“Stuff a few of them in your pockets to bring home to your wife. Maybe that will help ease her pain a little.”

On the way out of the caves, they headed back to get the baby. Moona was waiting there for them, tending to Matteus, who was cooing and smiling. She nodded at Calvin and told him again, with a small tear in her eye, how sorry she was.

Calvin stopped. “I understand how you felt about not being able to have a baby,” he said gently. “More than you know,” he told her. “But, if it means anything to you, I have faith. I mean…” he paused, trying to explain what he meant. “I will believe for you that, maybe someday, some way, you will have a baby of your own.” He said nothing more, but smiled compassionately at the pretty white wolf.

Just then they heard a sound, and Kanodia asked Calvin to stay with Moona for a moment while he went to check out what was happening.

Calvin couldn’t see where he had gone, but he certainly could hear it. Coming from somewhere close by, he heard Kanodia ordering Beast to give him the scepter.

“You’ll get nothing of the kind!” Beast raged, then he looked back at the hyenas and said, “And I’ll find out which one of you is the liar and the traitor!" he glared. "Pretending Kanodia was dead, you little rodents, you're gonna pay this time with your very lives, and then—" He stopped himself and turned back toward his enemy, Kanodia.

"I don't have time for your little foolish games. Just give me back what is mine," Kanodia demanded.

Beast raised his ugly head and swung it around toward the hyenas. "Seize him!" he roared. But none of the hyenas moved. They just stood there. Surprised and furious, Beast roared again, this time showing his long pointy fangs, "Seize him, you cowards! Or else!"

Two hyenas began to move toward Kanodia, but Kanodia grabbed them and flung them into the sky. Kanodia lobbed them in one swift swipe, then watched as they smashed, one after the other, into a tree and dropped. They screeched loudly as they crumpled like mere old rags onto a heap on the ground. The other hyenas stood there, motionless.

Kanodia looked at Beast straight in the eyes and said, "It's over, Beast. Now, give me the scepter! Quickly, before I tear you to pieces."

Then all that could be heard throughout the whole forest was screeching and banging, and the next thing they saw was a big, black, tailless, hyena flying through the sky and landing who knew where, with a screaming, smashing thud!

Just a short time later, Kanodia returned to Moona and Calvin, though he was a little out of breath. He said to them, "All set," then he thought a moment, "Oh, ah, I forgot something."

But as soon as he said it, the whole pack of hyenas were coming toward him, carrying the jeweled scepter. Kanodia was prepared, but then one of them stepped forward. "We are giving you back your scepter," they announced humbly, "and we want to thank you for getting rid of Beast for us. You see, we are glad he is gone!"

They handed him back his scepter, and the young hyena explained how he had taken it long ago and hidden it, knowing that Beast had wanted it more than anything, and the young hyena figured that he might need it someday, maybe even to save some of them from the torture and the wrath of the evil Beast.

Kanodia nodded and took back his scepter from the brave hyena. Then he turned his attention back to Calvin and Moona. "Well," he said, "things are starting to look up!" He smiled at Moona.

"Could you keep this for me, Moona, until I get back?" Kanodia asked her as he gave her the jeweled scepter.

Moona smiled and nodded, "That's my job!"

Then, as Kanodia had promised, he led Calvin and his son swiftly and safely home.

15
Believe

Crystalina sobbed with relief as Calvin carefully handed her the baby, while trying to explain to her about Moona and Kanodia. "But, as you can see, he's fine, honey."

He watched her coddle the baby with a look of pure elation on her face. He knew she wasn't even paying attention to what he said. She was so happy and relieved to have her baby back and so was he, but he couldn't resist saying, softly, "Yup, he's doing just great, and we're rich." Then he got up from his chair and went to the other room, leaving her to sing and rock the baby in the special rocking chair he had made for them.

In the morning, they began to pack up the house. There was no way that Calvin could leave them there alone ever again. But the good news was that now he didn't have to.

As Crystalina was packing up everything with her baby right by her side, she suddenly thought of what Calvin had said the night before and asked, "What do you mean *we're rich*?"

Calvin smiled at her, "Just what I said, hon. We're rich!" He let her wonder a minute while she looked at him strangely, and then he laughed and told her the whole story.

Crystalina was shocked, and all she kept saying as Calvin told the story was, "You're kidding," and, "you're joking," and, "*wow!*" He took the big, dazzling gems out of his pockets to show her a sample. She began jumping on the bed and laughing gleefully. "What started as a nightmare has turned out so, so fantastic!" As they packed, they laughed and talked and made plans for their future. They could fulfil their dreams, now, of having their own home in Morningstar, never having imagined it would come true so soon.

Calvin moved Crystalina and the baby into her parents' home again. Rose and Harry were thrilled to have them back with them, and they were very excited about Calvin finding the hidden diamonds that had been talked about longer than any of them could ever even remember.

When he knew they were safe and sound, he set off to the diamond mines to stake his claim.

Before Kanodia had left them at their door, he had actually given Calvin a code. It was a secret code; a way that Kanodia could hear him every time he entered into the forest. He was to take the rock that Kanodia had given him and bang it on another special rock that the wolf had shown him. It was three bangs to the left side of the rock, three on top of the rock, then one on the right side of the rock. Then, Kanodia had said, "Just say my name, and I'll be there!" And when Calvin went into the forest, he took the rock and banged out the code, said his name, and then he waited. The next thing Calvin heard was Kanodia saying, "You called?"

Four days later, Calvin returned to his wife and child a very rich man, and when he came through the door, he could not help but announce, "Let the fun begin!"[21]

Over the next few weeks, Calvin had purchased acres and acres of the finest land in Morningstar Village. Shortly after that, they began to build their dream house. Everything moved along very smoothly and quickly.

Once he had a home for his family, he built a home for Rose and Harry, and he also made a small, quaint, little house close to his own. He had hopes that maybe Mrs. Tag would come to Morningstar again, and possibly even stay.

Once all the homes were built, Calvin spared no expense in throwing a huge gala party. Almost everyone in the whole Village was invited to attend to celebrate their good fortune. They simply made signs and put them around the Village to let everyone know of the celebration. He even managed to get a message to Buxston Gizzard, who said he'd be glad to attend, "as long as Calvin was footin' da bill!"

The party was beautiful. They feasted and danced and sang. Everyone came to the party; the triplets were there with their sky-high hair, decked out in their new dresses. Calvin had made Biffer even richer by purchasing much of the land in Morningstar, so he was there, too. Buxston

[21] Electric Light Orchestra. "Starlight"

loved sitting with Dredge, and they found they had a lot in common. Even Dapper came to share in the fun as he walked in, decked out in black leather, with his wife by his side. Karess wore a long, bright, canary-yellow dress with a yellow feather in her hair.

As the night rolled on, Calvin told them all that he had wanted to make a toast. He called Hedda and Carlton to stand beside him, and handed them each a bag. They looked inside and found that it was full of diamonds! Calvin held up his drink and announced, "Finding a true friend is worth more than diamonds! But since that's all I can give these two guys who came to help me at one of the hardest times in my life, the diamonds will have to do!"

Everyone laughed and clapped. Hedda and Carlton were thrilled, and Calvin knew they had both wanted to have their own houses, and now, with the diamonds, they would be able to have that and their own land, too.

Calvin held up his glass. "Everyone, please, join me in a toast—to Hedda and Carlton, good friends!"

They all said, "Here, here!" and held up their glasses too, and drank.

The music began to play and filled the air around them as they danced. The celebration went on deep into the night with everyone having the very best of times of their lives. Meanwhile, there was another celebration going on deep in the forest. All the wolves were rejoicing over the return of their leader. That is, everyone except

Evana. She hung her head grimly during the whole celebration party.

Manny was more than happy to give Kanodia back his rightful place as leader of the pack. He even had their cave restored exactly the way it had been before Moona and Kanodia left. Best of all, even the jeweled scepter was displayed at the entryway of the cave.

Kanodia made an announcement that the Beast was dead! At first, there was silence. Everyone was unsure if they had heard him right. Beast had been such a threat to them for so long, but Kanodia announced again, "Did you all hear me? I'll say it louder, then. THE BEAST IS DEAD!"

Then everyone began to cheer and applaud and dance! Kanodia went on, after they finally quieted down, to tell them how even the hyenas were thrilled to be rid of their evil leader, and he had been able to come to an agreement with all of them, to live together in peace. Kanodia stopped talking as the wolves began to jump with glee. He nodded at them in agreement.

He then called on the young wolf, Seneca, to come to stand beside him. He announced proudly to all how brave the young wolf was, and gave him a blue Medal of Honor, while electing him to the third highest position, under Manny. He also asked all the wolves to join him in commending Manny for the outstanding job that he and his wife had done while he was gone. "If not for them," Kanodia announced, "there might not have been any pack to return to." Kanodia gave Manny the highest Golden Medal of Honor that can be awarded to any wolf. The wolves howled and applauded as Manny stood there before them and humbly thanked them all. Even Evana seemed to light up for a moment.

Moona's parents beamed in the audience, so elated and filled with relief and joy at seeing their daughter happy again and in her rightful place beside her husband, Kanodia.

Kanodia ended his speech by saying, "And I promise, things are gonna be great! Even better than they had ever been before," and he looked at Moona and whispered, "especially now, with you by my side once more."

The wolves celebrated for days with no end. They had never remembered being so unbelievably joyous! Kanodia and Manny even threw the hyenas a few of their roast beasts! The hyenas had never had it so good or eaten so well.

Life went along great for Calvin and Crystalina. Everyone around them seemed content and happy. Calvin was sometimes bothered, though, when he thought about Moona and the look on her face when Kanodia had told him they could not have a baby. He wished so much that somehow she could have her child, because he had seen that same look in his own wife's eyes so long ago, now. It had been such a blessing to them, such a miracle for them when they had their son, that he faithfully kept them in his prayers, believing that, someday, they would have a miracle too.

One night, Calvin woke abruptly in the early hours of the morning to a strange sound. He listened and thought it sounded like something was crying, and it seemed like it was coming from outside.

Quietly, he got dressed and slipped out the back door, trying not to wake anyone. It was barely light yet, but he could see a little. He walked into his back yard and followed the sound to the end of his land, where it ran into a river that flowed behind it, leading him toward the winter side of the Village.

As Calvin hurried along, the crying sound was getting louder, and as he looked down the river he saw that there, stuck on a branch in the fast-moving water, was a tiny wolf pup, crying for help.

Calvin saw in an instant the deer tracks and the wolf tracks that followed behind them. He whispered to himself, "The wolves must have been chasing a deer into the river, and it looks like they were all whisked away!" He didn't waste another moment, and ran to the river's edge to try to reach the baby wolf. He strained to reach him, and then stepped into the fast-moving water grabbing branches to keep him from being swept away. He leaned and quickly whisked the tiny wolf into his arms, and brought him into his house and wrapped it in a warm blanket. The tiny wolf was exhausted and fell asleep in Calvin's arms.

Later that day, when Crystalina woke, he told her what happened. He left the wolf with her while he went to investigate what happened to the wolf's parents. He walked along the riverbank for a long, long time. Soon, though, he found them lying on the river's edge, and Calvin knew it was too late for them. He gave them a proper burial and then he returned home.

When he got home, he sadly explained to Crystalina what had happened to the wolf's parents, but he knew what he was going to do about it, and when he told her, she agreed. Calvin scooped up the baby wolf again, still keeping the blanket around it. Then he headed back into the forest.

He decided not to call Kanodia. He felt he could find his way to the caves on his own. As he neared the caves, he covered the baby wolf's head, wanting to surprise them both. In a matter of minutes, Kanodia and Moona came running toward him and welcomed him.

"I have a gift, for both of you this time," he announced, smiling. Then he carefully laid down the little blanketed package he held and set it before them.

The wolves looked puzzled. Slowly, Calvin peeled back the blanket, and as soon as he did, a tiny, fluffy, baby wolf squirmed out and looked up at Moona.

Moona's blue eyes lit up with wonder as she looked at the little brown fur ball with the white patch around one eye. Calvin quickly explained what had happened the night before.

"You mean—he's mine?" Moona asked, barely getting the words out.

Calvin nodded and said, "He's yours forever, Moona, and I am only too thrilled in having the honor of bringing him to you!"

"I remember you told me that you believed it would happen for us one day! And look!" Moona cried as she stared joyfully at the little baby wolf.

He nodded and smiled at her. Calvin and Kanodia both watched Moona. It was as if a fire had been lit inside her heart again. It was a glow that came over her, and a sparkle that shown right through her eyes.

She went to the baby and he nuzzled right up to her, making little, soft baby sounds.

"He is the most beautiful thing I have ever seen," Moona told them. And it was in that very moment that Moona finally became a mother.

Calvin and Crystalina made so many plans for their family and also the people they would help. But first, Calvin wanted to do something that had been on his mind a lot.

He wrote a letter to Mrs. Tag, telling her that he had a big surprise for her, and asked her if she could stay for a while. He didn't tell her about the diamond mines. He was saving that little detail, and decided that would tell her if she were able to come.

He sat at his desk and thought for a long time about writing to his stepmother again, but in the end he figured it was no use. She had never returned any of his letters and he had tried many times. He decided that she must not want to hear from him.

Every now and then, Calvin would look out his window and see Kanodia, Moona and their baby that they had named Cally, after Calvin. Many times, Calvin, Crystalina and Matteus would take long walks with the wolves, and sometimes they all swam in the quarry or slid down the falls together. Calvin never would have imagined that one of his best friends would be a wolf.

A few weeks after sending Mrs. Tag a letter, he received a letter in the mail. At first, he thought it was from her, but then he realized it was from his stepmother.

He went off alone to the quarry to read the letter. It said:

Dear Calvin,

First, I want you to know that I have indeed received all of your letters. Admitting that, alone, makes me feel, as I am writing this letter, that it may be too late, since I never bothered to write to you before now. I really am unsure of where to begin to explain what I would like to say to you, so I guess I'll just start.

The twins have long since grown and left home for more schooling. It would be my utmost delight to be able to tell you how they are doing,, but I, myself, do not know that, since they hardly ever return home, preferring to go off with wealthy friends on weekends and school breaks, and I only hear from them when they have spent their allowances. I have written so many letters to them and even written to others that know them, trying to keep track of where they are and how they are really doing, but I just get vague responses every now and then.

Recently, well, I would say in the last six months or so, I started to get angry thinking about them. I was thinking how cold and unfeeling they were, and I wondered why they would treat me so inconsiderately and callously. Suddenly, in that moment, it came to my mind, for the very first time, that they were just like me! They were imitating the same behavior and attitudes that they had seen in me, because that's how they had seen me treat you.

Calvin, you must believe me when I say, in that minute, my heart just broke into pieces, because I suddenly realized how you must have felt! I understood how I must have made you feel so terribly alone. I now understand, too, why you probably couldn't wait to leave someone as cold as I had been toward you.

I have thought about this every day since then and I have felt nothing but remorse, shame, and regret. I just wanted to let you know that you were really a wonderful child, and a very caring adult. And I'm telling you this not just because you behaved well, but also because I know you really tried with me. I want to tell you how truly and deeply sorry that I am, Calvin, and to let you know that had your mother been able to watch you grow up, she would have been so very proud.

I only wish now that I had been better to you. I hope, in your travels and with your new marriage, that God will bless you doubly, maybe in some way he will make up to you for all the things I lacked.

I hope someday, maybe you can forgive me.

And then she signed it. *With love and respect, Mam.*

It took quite a few days for the letter from his stepmother to sink in. It had been such a drastic change in her, but then, finally, Calvin wrote back, and, for the first time, he felt like he could really be himself with her. He told her he was sorry about the twins, and hoped she would hear from them soon. He said he was glad to finally hear from her, and that her letter really meant a lot to him.

He told her about his baby boy. Then he told her of the diamond mines and said if she needed any financial help, he would be glad to give her whatever she needed.

He wrote on, saying that she was welcome to come and stay whenever she wished. He told her that it would mean a great deal to him if she were able to come someday. And not to worry, he, of course, had forgiven her.

He didn't know if she would ever come to Morningstar or not, but somehow, it was as if some kind of weight had been lifted off of his shoulders, and everything, everywhere, for the first time in his lifetime, felt right.

It was shortly after that day, that there was a knock on Calvin's front door. When he opened the door, there standing before him was Mrs. Tag. Calvin was thrilled, and as he hugged her, he called for Crystalina.

"Well!" exclaimed Mrs. Tag. "I can certainly see that the Good Lord has blessed you a hundred fold!" She began laughing. As Crystalina and the baby walked in, she said, "And look at this beautiful wife and child he has given you! Why, Calvin, I'm ready to start praisin' the Good Lord now for all I see he has gone and done for you!"

Calvin nodded his head, smiling, "You bet he has, and I have no doubt a lot of those blessings are probably due to your good prayers!"

They all sat down for dinner, and talked and ate and laughed for hours, and Crystalina loved her immediately, and so did Matteus. "Ya know, Calvin, I could tell from your letter that something good had happened. I'm tellin' you, maybe it was the Good Lord tellin' me something, but I just got the feeling, like goose bumps, that something real good was happening with you and I am just delighted to see that it has!"

"I'm just so glad to see you," he told her again, squeezing her hand across the dining table.

She looked like she was getting tears in her eyes as she grinned warmly back at him. "By the way, I bet I can guess that you made all the furnishings for this house. Why, I don't know what to look at first! It's all so lovely, so elegant, yet warm."

"Remember, I told you that I had a surprise for you. Well, here is one of them," he said as he slid the gift toward her. She gently opened the box, and inside was a beautifully cut, big diamond that dangled from a sparkling, golden chain.

"I had it made just for you," he told her.

"Oh, Calvin, I can't accept something as elaborate as this. Why, I never expected, in my wildest dreams—" She put her hand on her heart.

"Oh, yes, you most certainly can accept it, and you must. Think of it as a rock exchange." They laughed, remembering the rock Mrs. Tag had given him so long ago. "I wanted you to know how much I appreciated your encouragement and support. You were the one who inspired me to have faith and pursue what was in my heart. I may never have come here at all if not for you." He looked at her a moment and tapped her hand and said, "Follow me; I have something else for you."

He led her out across the back yard to the carriage house he had built for her. It was complete with a front porch and even a swing that faced the beautiful sunrise, which she had told him about so many years before.

"This is for you," he said. "It's yours forever, or as long as you want it." She was speechless, but he could see in her eyes she was thrilled. "Let's go in," he announced. "I hope you don't mind, but I took the liberty of furnishing it for you too."

As they walked through the house, and then all around the property, she told him, over and over, how thrilled she was with everything. "Why, I'm thrilled for you, and your wife, and your little baby! Why, I'm thrilled even for me!"

Calvin laughed, "I hope you will stay for a long time."

"Calvin," she said, "There is really no place on earth I'd rather be." Calvin smiled and gave her the key.

One evening, Calvin came in late, and ran upstairs to tell Crystalina the happy news. "Moona is going to have a baby!" he said joyfully. "Can you imagine, after all that they went through?"

Crystalina was so happy for them. "And I have some happy news." She added. "We are going to have another baby, too!" Calvin was elated.

Karess and Dapper did not have any children, though she had tried everything, even many new potions that the witch brewed up. It was no use, though; she could not even remember how old she really was anymore.

It was in the midnight hour, that Karess was startled from her sleep by an eerie sound. She sat up quickly, looking over at Dapper who slept on soundly. She went to the window. Though it was dark out, the moon held just enough light that she could see the two big black ravens, flying outside, circling like dark, threatening evil spirits. As if they knew she saw them, they let out the familiar screech. *"Rah! See the truth! See the truth!"* She gasped and stepped away. A feeling of utter dread and horror filled her; she knew this was a bad omen. She froze for a moment and reached up slowly to touch her face. Her skin felt strange to her, dry and saggy, *but she had just had her youth potion a few days ago*, she thought.

She ran out of the room quickly, fearing Dapper would wake up and see her. She raced to find a mirror. As she stared at her reflection, she remembered the words of the man on the donkey, when he had warned her, *'you are using powers of utter darkness, and in the end they will completely destroy you!'*

She stared at the side of her face. It was true, the witch had tricked her! The whole side of her lovely face had begun to age and wither![22]

Dapper woke to her screams. He ran to find her, but she had already run out of the house and into the forest where he could see a dark, thick, fog rolling into the night. Days and weeks went by, but she didn't return.

Dapper was frantic, and rallied together many search parties, but after searching all through the forest night and day, everyone finally told him it was no use. She was nowhere to be found.

---

[22] Aerosmith. "Seasons of Wither"

Everyone in the Village wondered what had happened to her. There were many rumors, but the most reliable people said that she had gone back into the forest to see the witch. When she got there, the witch's house had burned to the ground. There was nothing left but smoke and ashes. People claimed that, in the dark of the night, they could hear the agonizing screams and sobs of Karess coming from the deep woods. Someone even said they had seen her running through the forest and then disappearing again, as if she were hiding.

Finally Dapper's sorrow grew unbearable; he feared what could be happening to her. He looked for her everywhere. He could not give up; he decided he would never give up. He packed a few items, and left a letter for his family telling them he would not return to Morningstar without her.

The people of the Village talked about it constantly, wondering if she was an old hag now, or if she was even *alive.* Some still went out to search for them, but it seemed they were nowhere to be found.

Then one night, in the ninth week of his absence, under a full moon, someone caught a glimpse of a man coming out of the forest, carrying someone wrapped in a blanket. It was Dapper, carrying Karess! She was wrapped tightly and her face was hidden. "*She's fading fast*" he told someone.

He carried her back to their home and the Doctor was called in. Dapper paced outside the door, desperately waiting for the Doctor to tell him if she could be saved.

The Doctor finally came out, looking shocked himself and shaking his head. He said, "She's aging quickly. I'm sorry, but there is nothing that can be done. It won't be much longer. I'm truly, very sorry."

Dapper stayed by her bedside night and day. He slept in the chair beside her bed not wanting to disturb her rest or her small, frail body.

One morning in the pre-dawn hour, he woke up to hear her trying to say something. He rushed to kneel at her bedside; he leaned in close, straining to hear her faint whispers. She was so small, so unrecognizable now.

In a tiny, frail whisper, it took her last ounce of strength to say her final words. *"Thank you, thank you for lovin' me."* She winced in pain as she tried to take a breath, she went on *"In all the* many, *many years of my life, no one else eva did. And it took all this time to realize, that's all I eva really wanted."* She closed her eyes for the last time.

Dapper put his head down and wept.

Calvin looked out over the vast land, and all that God had given him. A rush of emotion filled him as he recalled what the minister had said that day so long ago.

'He will make all things work for good to those that believe in him.'

For Calvin, God had not even missed the smallest detail, and had answered all his prayers, even in such a way that it was more than he could even have ever dreamed possible.

Suddenly, he knew what he needed to do next. As he watched his little boy toddle through the grass, he picked him up and sat him on his lap. Calvin pointed toward Heaven and began to tell Matteus all he had learned.

He told him, "Son, I want you to know that God has a great plan for your life..."

Epilogue

Grandpa Matteus closed the journals and looked over at his grandson, Harry, who was still wide-awake.

"Wow," exclaimed Harry.

Grandpa smiled warmly. "So, now you know, Harry, that we owe your Great, Great Grandfather Calvin a lot. You see, if it were not for his character, courage, and faith, we might not be here today. I want you to know you can be proud of your family and your heritage, and I hope that you will remember the example he set for us."

"How could I ever forget it? He was really awesome!" Harry sat up. "But, I have a couple questions."

"Yes, Harry?"

"So, was your dad Matteus, Calvin's son?"

Grandpa nodded, "Yes, Harry. Matteus, the one who was taken by Kanodia when he was a baby, was my father, and he was your great grandfather."

"I knew it! That's why you have the same name. Oh, wow, grandpa. That is totally amazing." Said Harry. "And Crystalina, did she have another baby?"

Grandpa nodded again. "She sure did, she had a baby girl that they named Constance, after Calvin's mother, who he had sadly lost when he was very young."

"I'll never forget this, Grandpa. I'll always remember Great, Great Grandfather Calvin and what a good man he was, and I will never forget you, Grandpa, and how lucky I am to have you." Harry smiled up at his grandfather as he reached to give him a hug. "You and Great, Great Grandpa Calvin are the best, and I want to be just like both of you!"

Grandpa smiled. "Oh, and that reminds me, Moona finally had her baby too. It was a girl, and they named her Serenity, and she was white as snow, just like her mother," he told him as he patted his grandson on the head.

Harry smiled up at his grandfather. "I'm really, really happy to hear that everything turned out so great for all of them. Thank you, Grandpa, for sharing the story with me." He whispered as his eyes began to close. "Goodnight, Grandpa."

"Goodnight, Harry, and remember to hang on to those dreams!"

Grandpa returned the old journals to the safe. He carefully put in the combination and waited to hear it click. He laid the journals inside, but couldn't resist pulling out the jeweled rock his father had given him so long ago. It was from Morningstar's jeweled streets. He admired each unique layer. Then he pulled out the glass case that held the 10 carat diamond he had inherited. There, it was dazzling in all its sparkling glory. His great grandfather, Calvin, had wanted him to have it, and one day he would give it to his own grandson. He smiled to himself, *I bet Calvin would have really liked that.*

Music Bibliography

“Grandpa”, written by Jamie O’Hara; performed by The Judds

“To Make You Feel My Love”, written by Bob Dylan; performed by Garth Brooks

“By My Side”, written by Peggy Gordon and Jay P. Hamburger; performed by Peggy Gordon

“Father And Son”, written and performed by Cat Stevens

“Spirit In The Sky”, written and performed by Norman Greenbaum

“Big Wheels”, written by Jeff Lynne; performed by Jeff Lynne and Electric Light Orchestra

“Lagrange”, written by Dusty Hill, Billy F Gibbons, Frank Lee Beard; performed by ZZ Top

“Up, Up And Away”, written by Jimmy Layne Webb; performed by The Fifth Dimension

“Locomotive Breath”, written by Ian Anderson; performed by Jethro Tull

“Man After Your Own Heart”, written and performed by Gary Chapman

“Black Magic Woman”, written by Peter Green; performed by Santana

“Natural High”, written by Charles McCormick; performed by Bloodstone

"Why Not Me", written by Harlan Howard, Sonny Throckmorton, and Brent Maher; performed by The Judds

"Can't Find The Time", written by Bruce Arnold; performed by Orpheus

"Believe Me Now", written by Jeff Lynne; performed by Jeff Lynne and Electric Light Orchestra

"Question 67 & 68", written by Robert Lamm; performed by Chicago

"Never My Love", written by Donald and Richard Addrisi; performed by The Fifth Dimension

"One In A Million You", written by Sam Dees; performed by Larry Graham

"Dialogue", written by Robert Lamm; performed by Chicago

"Standin' In The Rain", written by Jeff Lynne; performed by Electric Light Orchestra

"Starlight", written by Jeff Lynne; performed by Electric Light Orchestra

"Seasons Of Wither", written by Steven Tyler; performed by Aerosmith